STOWAWAY TO AMERICA

Books by BORGHILD DAHL

GLIMPSES OF NORWAY

I WANTED TO SEE

HOMECOMING

THE DAUGHTER

THE CLOUD SHOES

KAREN

STOWAWAY TO AMERICA

Stowaway to America

by BORGHILD DAHL

NEW YORK   E. P. DUTTON & COMPANY, INC.   1959

Library of Congress Catalog Card Number: 59-5847

TO MY NIECES,
MARGARET, JUNE AND DALE
AND MY NEPHEW DAVID

STOWAWAY TO AMERICA

In 1825 a group of about forty Norwegians left their native land to escape religious persecution. In the Restoration, a tiny sailing vessel a quarter the size of the Mayflower, they made an heroic three-month voyage across the Atlantic. Near Rochester, New York, these stanch dissenters, under the inspired leadership of Cleng Peerson, established the first permanent Norwegian colony in America.

CHAPTER ONE

Margit stood outside the parlor door and was about to open it, when she heard Master Cleng's name mentioned. She waited. He was coming home from America, Carrie Nelson said. Margit held her breath. This was real news! Master Cleng had been away for almost three years now, and if anyone had heard from him, she had not been told. Mistress Catherine was not in the habit of telling her servants anything.

Carrie Nelson was making an unexpected call on her sister-in-law this afternoon and Mistress Catherine was having coffee served in the parlor. Margit had forgotten the coffee cozy and porcelain coffeepot and Mistress Catherine had sent her out to the kitchen to get it.

"You can see by the letter that he intends to return soon," Carrie Nelson said.

After that her voice dropped. Both women spoke in low tones, and Margit could not hear what they were saying. Besides, Mistress Catherine might come out at any moment to find out what was keeping her.

As Margit served the coffee, she could not help noticing the contrast between the sisters-in-law. Carrie Nelson was plump and her blond hair refused to stay in place. Margit had the impression that her clothes, though scrupulously clean, had been put on in a hurry. Mistress Catherine's skin was dark and sallow. Her deep-set eyes, her high forehead and her thin lips made her face appear much longer than it really was. Margit had never seen her without the purple wool scarf with which she covered her hair. Her entire body was made up of such sharp angles that they showed through the mounds of clothing which she wore, winter and summer. In disposition they were different, too. There always seemed to be a smile on Carrie Nelson's lips. Mistress Catherine almost never smiled.

Margit lingered in the parlor, hoping that she might learn a little more about Master Cleng's home-coming. She filled and refilled Mistress Catherine's and Carrie Nelson's coffee cups and passed the plate of cakes again and again. This last caused her some misgivings, for with the gradual dwindling of the cakes on the plate down to five, then four and finally to one, Margit's hopes for a little treat for herself and Ingrid, the young girl who worked with her in the kitchen, were gone. But still Margit stayed on.

At last Mistress Catherine said, "You may remove the tray, Margit."

There was nothing she could do. She had to leave.

Once outside the door, Margit was tempted to stay and find out whether the women resumed their earlier conversation. But no. Eavesdropping by accident was one thing. Deliberately setting out to listen for what was evidently not meant for one's ears was something else.

In the kitchen, Ingrid was eagerly awaiting Margit's return. As Margit set the tray down on the workbench, Ingrid received the empty plate with an expression of keen disappointment.

"Yes, they ate them all," Margit said. "But I've got news for you, Ingrid."

Ingrid regarded Margit with surprise. "What is it?" she asked eagerly.

For many months now, the two young girls had worked together in Mistress Catherine's huge, dark, gloomy kitchen. Since the annual Christmas Eve feast, when servants, cottagers and their families on the estate gathered at Mistress Catherine's manor house, there had not been the slightest bit of excitement on the place. Ingrid, who was the daughter of one of the cottagers, went home nights to sleep. But with the long working hours and the darkness and the cold, she had been able to bring little from the outside world.

Now it was late March and spring was in the air. Carrie Nelson had come to call. And she had brought news.

"Tell me quickly, Margit, what did you hear?"

"I'll give you three guesses," Margit teased.

"The Nelsons have lost another cow. It was last year this time their best one was drowned."

"You're wrong. Guess again."

"The Nelsons are going to have another baby."

"Wrong again. If they were, Carrie Nelson wouldn't tell Mistress Catherine before she had to. She told Carrie last time they already had too many mouths to feed."

"I give up. Tell me, Margit."

Margit could not resist the pleading in Ingrid's voice. "Master Cleng is coming home!"

Ingrid let out a yell of joy.

"Better not make so much noise," Margit cautioned her. "Mistress Catherine will be out here to find out what the trouble is."

"When is he coming? What else did you hear?"

"Carrie Nelson said soon. He wrote a letter—I guess it was either to her or to their brother."

"What else?"

"That's all. But isn't that enough?"

"Of course. I can't wait to tell Mother about Master Cleng's return," Ingrid said. "If it wasn't for him, she wouldn't have let me work here. He has always been so kind to all of us. And Father says that the lot of the cottagers has been much better since Mistress Catherine married him."

"I know. I'd die if Master Cleng didn't come home from his travels once in a while," Margit said.

Ingrid started removing dishes from the tray. "It's so dark here over by the workbench that I'm almost afraid to handle these fragile dishes," she said. "I wish I dared to light a candle."

"You'd better not. Gunda might come in at any moment. And you know how she is about carrying out Mistress Catherine's every whim."

"You can dry them for me. You won't soil your best dress doing that."

For a while the two girls worked in silence. Margit could think of nothing but the wonderful news she had just heard— that Master Cleng was coming home. And even though Carrie Nelson had not been able to give the exact time, she thought it would be soon.

As far back as Margit could remember, Master Cleng had brought into her life whatever real sunshine she had ever known. When she was a very little girl, he had carried her piggyback around the estate, letting her see and pet the tiny animals down at the barns and in the sheep shed, holding her so low that she could watch the fish swimming in the brook down by the dairy. In winter, he pulled her on a sled he had made for her and sometimes sat on it himself, holding her in his lap and steering it down the high hill on which the manor house was situated.

When she was a little older, they walked together around the place, and although she was not able to grasp all he told her, she learned a lot. He explained what grew in the fields, he brought her into Hans Skomaker's harness and shoemaker shop and let her watch Hans tan leather, cut it out and sew it into harnesses and shoes. He explained about tools in his carpenter shop, and they paid visits to the dairy and the smoke shed and other outbuildings below the high hill.

Best of all, they spent hours together in the beautiful arbor where, seated on a bench, he told her countless stories. She called it the tree house because the walls and ceiling were really nothing but vines climbing on trellises. Master Cleng had intended it for an outside tea and dining room for the family during fine weather, but Mistress Catherine had refused to have food dragged out into a drafty place when she had a perfectly good house to eat in.

As soon as Margit was able to help Gunda in the kitchen, and could knit and spin, all these pleasure jaunts of her very early childhood ceased. And Master Cleng's travels grew more and more frequent and he stayed away longer. Now he had been gone for almost three years and she had begun to fear he would never return.

Margit remembered with a pang how dark and dismal the kitchen seemed to her the first time Mistress Catherine refused to allow her to go with Master Cleng on one of his jaunts around the estate. The dark-brown ceiling and walls and the dark-stained floor seemed to close in around her like a prison. The corners of the huge room were like caverns. As she stood by the fire, stirring a pot Gunda had told her to watch, and the smoke rose in a cloud up into her face, she felt she couldn't breathe. From that day to the present time, she had had to watch the sunshine through that one small window in Mistress Catherine's kitchen.

If it hadn't been for Ingrid, the years would have seemed much longer and much drearier. She was kind and capable and full of fun. They got along famously. Since Ingrid had come to work at Mistress Catherine's, Master Cleng had teased her and joked with her just as he did with Margit. And on his return from his travels, he gave her presents just as he did Margit.

What gifts would he have for them this time on his return from America, Margit wondered, as she continued to dry the precious porcelain coffee service. The tiny tinkling bell he had brought her from Germany and the silk kerchief from France were still in her box of treasures on the shelf in her cupboard up in her room.

Margit's thoughts were interrupted by the opening of the door leading to the entry. Gunda, weighed down by two large pails, came into the kitchen. Breathing hard, she set them on one end of the workbench, and started to brush her gray wool homespun dress that had become damp from the drizzle outside.

"We're using the milk in one of the pails for the porridge at the evening meal," she said hoarsely. "Pour the other into the cheese vat. I'm starting a batch this afternoon."

Margit was about to bend down to get the vat that was kept behind all the other pots and pans under the workbench.

"Let me do it," Ingrid said. "I have my old clothes on."

She got down on her knees, and after removing most of the contents of the low cupboard, she took out the vat.

"Here it is," she said, replacing the pots and pans.

At that moment, a boy of about thirteen years of age came in through the open entry door.

Gunda turned toward him. "What do you want?" she demanded. Because of the absence of two front teeth, her words came out slightly slurred.

"Mother said for me to ask you if Ingrid could come home early tonight. It's Alf's birthday and he's so small that he'd fall asleep if we waited too long to cut the *geburtsdagskringle*. And mother would also like Ingrid to be home to help sing the birthday verses that she and I have made up for him."

"The Mistress doesn't think much of such foolishness," Gunda said sourly.

"That's not foolishness," Margit said. "I wish we celebrated everybody's birthday here. It would be lots of fun. You'd like it too, Gunda, once we got started."

"It's the first time I've asked to leave early," Ingrid said. "And often it's late before I get started—"

"You'll have to get permission from the Mistress," Gunda said firmly. "You ought to know better, Margit, than to encourage Ingrid in such foolishness. I, for one, will certainly not be responsible for it."

Margit put her hand on Ingrid's shoulder affectionately. "Never mind, Ingrid," she said. "I'll go and ask Mistress Catherine to let you go, and I won't give up until she has given her consent." She turned to Ingrid's brother. "Wait here until I get back."

Margit walked quickly down the hall. She hoped Carrie Nelson had left, for she didn't want her to get involved, should there be an argument. Mistress Catherine felt edgy enough toward her sister-in-law as it was. But Margit would have to risk that. When she reached the parlor door this time, she knocked without the slightest hesitation.

"Who's there? What do you want?" The tone of Mistress Catherine's voice did not sound too promising.

Without waiting for an invitation, Margit walked in. "Ingrid's mother has sent word that she would like to have Ingrid come home early," Margit said, coming to the point at once, since she saw that Mistress Catherine was alone.

"Why should the girl have to do that?" Mistress Catherine demanded.

"It's her little brother Alf's birthday and he'd be unable to stay up late enough to cut his *geburtsdagskringle* if she came home at the usual time. And her mother would like her to sing the verses she and her older brother have made up for the occasion."

"Such foolishness. No wonder the cottagers are never prosperous, making up and singing nonsensical verses when they should be working."

"I'll do Ingrid's work for her."

"You have your own work to do."

"I'll do that, too. If it takes all night, I'll keep on until everything is done and well done."

"Oh, all right," Mistress Catherine said grudgingly. "Tell Gunda to let her go. But see to it that your fine words are followed by fine deeds."

"I will," Margit said, turning to go.

"Wait," Mistress Catherine commanded. "Ingrid must make up tomorrow the time she loses today."

"I will tell her," Margit said and hurried out before she had to hear any more.

When Margit returned to the kitchen, Ingrid and her brother greeted her with anxious glances. "What did she say? Will she let me go?" Ingrid asked.

"Yes, it's all right for you to leave," Margit said. Ingrid's eyes shown with gratitude. No use to spoil her pleasure by delivering Mistress Catherine's message, Margit thought.

"I'll be shorthanded," Gunda said glumly.

Ingrid, who had finished washing the dishes during Margit's absence, dried her hands. Then she took her jacket from the peg on the wall in the entry where it had been hanging and put it on. Margit went outside with Ingrid and her brother.

"Greet the birthday child for me," she said gaily. "Sing a verse from me to him, too. Eat a piece of *geburtsdagskringle* for me. And all of you have a wonderful celebration!"

In spite of her brave words, Margit watched a little wistfully as the two walked down the path. As she told Gunda, it would have been so nice for everyone in Mistress Catherine's household to celebrate birthdays, too.

When Margit returned to the kitchen, Gunda walked heavily over to the fireplace at the far end of the room and started to stir vigorously the mixture in the cheese vat. "See to it that there is no more dawdling," she told Margit. "Get into your old clothes. You should have changed as soon as you finished serving the coffee in the parlor."

Margit went up to her room and did as she was told. It was cold and cheerless up there. The dark grayish blue of the ceiling and walls and the floor did little for the dim light which the one small window let in. Mistress Catherine had even insisted that Master Cleng use the same color on the cupboard because it would wear well. She had been angry when she discovered the blue bird in a cluster of gay flowers and green leaves painted on each of the doors. Margit took off her company apron, folded it carefully and put it on the shelf in the cupboard beside her box of treasures. She hung her best dress on one of the pegs below the shelf. Shivering, she put on her old dress and apron. It was almost dark by this time, but there were no shades to pull here. Only in the parlor where the sunshine had to be shut out would Mistress Catherine permit such luxury. Glancing around the room to see that everything was in order, in case Mistress Catherine came in to inspect—the narrow bed was the only other piece of furniture in the room and that was neatly made—Margit hurried down into the kitchen. She had scarcely closed the hall door when there was a sharp ring.

"Go into the parlor and see what the Mistress wants," Gunda said.

Again Margit did as she was told.

"Get me my shawl and wrap it around my shoulders," Mistress Catherine said. "I am completely tired out, what with entertaining Carrie Nelson this afternoon and all the other demands that are made on me."

Once more Margit did as she was told.

When Margit returned to the kitchen, Gunda asked, "What did the Mistress want?"

"Her shawl."

"She always freezes when she is tired. I wish her husband's family would not make so many demands on her."

Margit bit her lip, but said nothing. Gunda told Margit to stir the mixture in the cheese vat, while she busied herself with something out in the entry. As Margit stood over the fire, smoke rising up into her eyes and her hand aching from constant stirring, she gave way to self-pity. Was ever any girl worse off than she was? Destined to work day in and day out in a huge, dark, gloomy kitchen with such a dull, plodding person as Gunda who knew no better than to make it her one concern to humor every whim of Mistress Catherine. Even Ingrid was much better off than Margit. Although her family lived much more humbly than anyone in Mistress Catherine's household, there was love and happiness in their home in spite of their extreme poverty.

Ingrid's father and mother made their three children feel that they were the loveliest, the cleverest, the most important people to them in the entire world. Ingrid's father took them fishing in the nearby stream, took them for tramps in the woods and, during the winter, skiing with him up in the high

hills—all with their mother's consent and blessing. And Ingrid's mother called her "my treasure" and kissed her every
time she left for work. Margit could never remember having
been kissed.

Margit jerked the spoon she was stirring with so hard that
boiling cheese spilled into the fire. She set her lips firmly together and put her head back. She wouldn't accept this fate
without doing something about it. She'd free herself from
this drab, toilsome life of an unloved, unwelcome, dependent
drudge in Mistress Catherine's kitchen. She'd find some way
out. She wouldn't let the years slip by until she found herself
in the pitiful state Gunda had reached. Years ago Gunda, too,
must have been young and perhaps fairly good-looking. Margit had heard that she had been brought up by the mother of
Mistress Catherine's first husband. This woman must have demanded complete servility of Gunda and deprived her of all
spirit. And Mistress Catherine had certainly not helped to
change things for the poor creature.

She herself had had just about the same start as Gunda,
except that her early years, when Master Cleng was at home
more, had been softened by his kindness.

Mistress Catherine often said that she inherited Gunda, one
orphan, and the second one her present husband had inflicted
upon her because he was the child's godfather and had promised at the death of her parents to give her a Christian upbringing. But, since Cleng was gone so much of the time, this
burden had naturally fallen on her shoulders. Margit had to
admit that Mistress Catherine had not neglected her duty as
she had seen it. She had seen to it that Margit had been in-
formed in lurid detail of the horrible consequences if she
broke any of the Ten Commandments. She had been excused
only once from attending services at church, only because at
that time she was completely broken out with the measles. In

Margit's hearing, people often spoke of the great Christian virtue of a woman like Mistress Catherine, who had not only continued to give a good home to one orphan after she was too old to be of any real help, but also had taken upon herself the upbringing of another, a mere infant, who must have been a great care. They praised Mistress Catherine even more for having given Margit instructions in reading and writing, in order that she might be able to get at first hand the teachings of the Bible.

As Margit thought of all these remarks now, her eyes blurred from the smoking fire, and as she stirred the steaming cheese in the vat, they infuriated her more than ever.

Real parents weren't forever being praised for what they did for their children. No one mentioned the sacrifices Carrie Nelson, with the very limited means of her family, made for her children. Nor the loving care Ingrid's mother showered upon Ingrid and her two brothers. At this moment, Margit wished that she were a member of any household but Mistress Catherine's.

Gunda returned from the entry. "You let the cheese boil over," she said accusingly as she lumbered across the long kitchen floor. "I heard it sizzle into the fire."

"A little of it spilled when the ladle slipped in my hand," Margit said.

"See that it doesn't happen again. And don't let it scorch. You'll have to stay up and finish it tonight and clear up the kitchen after the evening meal. The rheumatism in my back is so bad I'm going straight up to bed."

It was hours later, after Margit had served the evening meal to Mistress Catherine and the servants, cleared up the kitchen and poured the cheese into containers to cool, that she went upstairs. When she lit the sputtering candle in her room it seemed colder and more desolate than ever. It took some time before her body warmed the bed enough to make it comfortable to lie in. And long after that she remained wide awake. She wondered whether Gunda had been able to sleep or if the pain of her rheumatism was bothering her too much. She'd like to get up and go into her room and ask her, but Gunda would only scold her for prowling about at night and disturbing the Mistress.

What really went on in Gunda's mind? How did she feel? How could she stand it, year in and year out, going down into the kitchen in the morning, slaving all day, and trudging dead tired and aching up to her cold and cheerless bedroom at night? Lately she had begged off from attending church on Sundays because her back and legs ached so she couldn't sit still and listen to the service.

The more Margit thought of Gunda, the more pity she felt for her. But the greater grew the dread of suffering a similar fate if she, too, continued to slave in Mistress Catherine's kitchen. Margit shivered. The mere thought of it was so frightening that she huddled down into the bed and tried to shut it out of her mind.

CHAPTER TWO

Margit woke up at least every hour during the night. Each time she thought, Master Cleng will be home tomorrow. In her mind, she pictured exactly how he would look. He would be wearing his fur cap, which remained on his head winter and summer, his gray wool shirt, his long black cloak and his high boots. His sideburns would be cut at an angle and there would be a gleam of mischief in his blue eyes.

Margit knew exactly what the sound of his voice would be like. After his first greeting, there would be a teasing quality in it as he asked, "Well, how has the young one been behaving?" But he wouldn't wait for an answer from either her or Mistress Catherine. Instead he would start right off telling some story about the adventures he had experienced during his travels. And what adventures! With a ring of excitement in his voice he would begin, "Child, in France, I came upon the most amazing incident. There was a young girl and her brother and the cleverest dog you ever saw. Wouldn't you like to have me tell you about it?"

Margit chuckled. Master Cleng had been gone so long this time, far across the Atlantic Ocean to America. That, in itself, was as exciting as any fairy tale. She would beg him to tell her no end of stories to make up for all she had missed.

In the morning she found that a complete change had taken place in the kitchen. A huge table had been brought in and set for many people. Gunda was hovering over steaming pots that hung above a bright fire in the hearth, and Ingrid was rushing around obeying Gunda's commands.

"Master Cleng arrived home during the night," Ingrid told Margit excitedly. "Mistress Catherine is having all the servants in to eat breakfast with her and Master Cleng." As she came closer, she lowered her voice. "It was Master Cleng who wanted it, and she couldn't very well refuse his first request."

Gunda turned from the fire. "You're late, Margit," she snapped.

"What would you like to have me do?" Margit asked politely.

"Get out the flat bread and some cakes from the hall cupboard. Mistress Catherine has already made her rounds to unlock things for the day." Then she turned to Ingrid. "You run down to the dairy and fetch a pitcher full of the best sweet cream."

As Margit flew about the kitchen doing Gunda's bidding, there was a song in her heart. "Master Cleng is home. Master Cleng is home."

The door from the hall suddenly opened. There he was exactly as she had pictured him except that the fur cap and the long black cloak were missing. There was another difference, too. His skin was a deep tan, as though he had been out in the hot sun.

Master Cleng put out his hand. "Well, how has the young one been. . . ." He stopped short. "But why. . . ." He hesitated. "Surely this beautiful young lady can't be the little girl I left behind?"

"Even in Norway time doesn't stand still." Mistress Catherine had entered the kitchen. "Margit is old enough to assume the duties of a grown woman. She is no longer a gullible child to be taken in by your wild tales."

Master Cleng chuckled. "Do you know, Catherine, she reminds me of some of the fine young ladies in New York."

Mistress Catherine scowled. "Margit, go outside. We have invited all the household for breakfast in honor of my husband's home-coming. Tell them we are ready to eat."

Margit darted out the entry door. She could easily wait to hear more of what Master Cleng had to tell about America. Master Cleng would have to give her her present later. Usually he waited until no one else was around and then slipped whatever he had for her into her hand. "It is perhaps best that you don't mention this to anyone for a little while," he would say. Mistress Catherine didn't find out about the bell until a year after she had received it, and then only when Margit had rung it, thinking no one else was in the house. Mistress Catherine had not been pleased at all, but since it really belonged to Margit, her conscience had not allowed her to take what was not hers.

It was a joyful group that sat down around the breakfast table. The special treat of a bountiful meal meant much to everyone, but the home-coming of their beloved Master Cleng meant even more. His return from the distant and fabulous America was something to be remembered all the rest of their lives.

"Was it really as large and wonderful a country as people say?" Margit asked.

"Much larger and much more wonderful," Master Cleng responded enthusiastically.

"I wonder what a person would notice first that was different from Norway," Margit continued.

Mistress Catherine gave Margit a disapproving glance, but today Margit did not mind.

"That is simple," Master Cleng said promptly. "The very first thing I noticed when I got off the ship in America was the naturalness and friendliness of everyone I met on the street." He turned toward Mistress Catherine as he went on speaking. "Just imagine, Catherine, what would happen to a person here in Norway, if, when he met a church or government official, he failed to bow almost to the ground and address him as though he were some sort of god or at least his lord and master here on earth. Well, in America there just isn't any such silly class distinction. You don't have to say, 'Yes, Your Honor, Mr. Bishop,' or 'Of course, Your Honor, Mr. Government Official and Madam Government Official.' You just address them as plain Mr. and Mrs. So and So. If I happened to meet the President of the United States, it would make no difference. All people in America are treated alike."

"Poor manners are no credit to any nation," Mistress Catherine said caustically.

Master Cleng emptied his cup of coffee and then he went on, "It was really a great relief not to have to remember titles in America. People over there have more important things to think about. The minute a poor emigrant from Europe sets foot on American soil, he suddenly feels himself an important human being. It must be something in the air, I guess."

"To me, lumping together princes and paupers into one class is disgusting," Mistress Catherine said.

"And the ladies in America, Catherine, are the most wonderful and charming creatures on God's earth."

"Did they wear beautiful clothes?" Margit asked.

"I wish all of you could have seen them promenading in the park along the water front of New York City. I don't know much about women's clothes, but they seemed to be wearing dresses of all the colors of the rainbow and they carried parasols to match. If I had been a better judge of materials—the dresses these women wore were made of some sort of fine thin stuff—I should have liked to have bought you complete outfits like theirs."

Mistress Catherine raised her eyebrows and opened her mouth as if to speak but she seemed to think better of it and went on cracking the shell of her second egg.

"Everyone in America can get rich in no time, if he really tries," Master Cleng continued. "I met Swedes, Danes, English and Frenchmen, Germans and people from many other countries. They all had the same story to tell. They had all arrived in America with both hands empty. In no time, after living in America, they started to forge ahead by leaps and bounds. They could buy fine clothes to wear and they owned their homes and they had stored away comfortable sums of money in the bank."

Mistress Catherine cleared her throat.

"You'd be especially interested, Catherine, to know that women in America did not think only of dressing beautifully. Especially Norwegian women. I could sit here from now until Christmas telling about their wonderful successes over there, and then I would not have had time to mention them all. Take for instance the case of Anne Jensen. She and her husband came from Norway to America and settled on a sixty-three-acre plot of ground on Manhattan Island. The place was nothing but a wilderness at the time, yet the two of them cultivated their farm so that it yielded rich harvests to them. Eventually it came to be a very valuable piece of land. In fact, their land now lies in the heart of New York City, and the famous Trinity Church and its surrounding churchyard, where many of America's most famous people are buried, are at the present day located on the very spot where Anne Jensen and her husband first settled. Think of the many generations that have toiled and sweated on this estate, and for all that, it is probably not worth a *krone* more than it was to its original owner."

"I have no ambition to convert this place into a cemetery," Mistress Catherine said dryly.

"But listen some more, Catherine. A narrow strip of their land—it was originally only a lane on their farm—is now called Wall Street and is known for its wealth throughout the world and for the tremendous amount of business that is transacted there. People say that you can hear the jingle of American silver dollars rolling down the cobblestones!"

Margit gasped. Her coffee cup dropped from her hand and left a dark brown stain on the snow-white linen table-cloth.

Ingrid was on her feet in an instant and came over to Margit's side. She placed her own napkin carefully over the blotch. Then, speaking in a low voice, yet loud enough for Mistress Catherine to hear, she said, "There isn't even a crack in the cup. And right after breakfast, I'll wash out the cloth with some of the extra fine soap Gunda made yesterday. There won't be a trace of the stain left."

Mistress Catherine, who had been regarding Margit with stern disapproval, now turned toward her husband once more. "Remember that we are responsible for every word that drops from our lips," she said. "Besides, how can you sit and put such nonsense into the head of the orphan whom God has entrusted to us?"

Master Cleng smiled. "Those tales are closer to the truth than you think. The story of Anne Bendicksdatter from Bergen is even more spectacular. Every detail I am going to tell you about her is absolute fact. She was a maiden lady

when she migrated to America, but she married a man from
Holland by the name of Jan Arentzen van der Bill. The two
of them became very prosperous and now their name is Van-
derbilt. The couple and their descendants became one of the
wealthiest families in the United States."

"And how many years did it take this beautiful, wonderful
Norwegian-American woman to accomplish so much?" Mistress Catherine asked. Then, without waiting for an answer,
she said, "We shall keep God waiting no longer. We have
already sinned this morning by breaking our fast without
asking His blessing. Gunda leave everything until after morning worship."

For the Scripture passage, Mistress Catherine read the story
of the Prodigal Son. In her prayer she asked that the members
of her household remember the gifts God had bestowed upon
them, to keep from reaching out beyond what He knew was
best for them. Then, before anyone else had a chance to speak,
she rose from her chair and said, "Thank you all for coming
to this meal, honoring my husband." With that, she walked
quickly toward the door leading to the front hall. The door
closed behind her.

Immediately everyone rose from the table, crowded about
Master Cleng and started at once to talk to him. Did he really
prefer the United States to Norway? Would he ever return
there? How could one who had always lived at Tysvaer go
about making arrangements to migrate, should he take a notion to do so? Was it terribly expensive to cross the Atlantic?
Did he have any idea of how a person might accumulate
enough *kroner* to pay for one's passage?

To these questions Master Cleng replied that he would
have to think before he could answer any of them. For a
while at least he would remain on the estate. If any one of
them were really interested in migrating, let him speak to

him individually. Leaving Norway was a crucial decision for a person to make. On the other hand, America offered opportunities that were unheard of and undreamed of in Norway.

For days after Master Cleng's return, Margit tried in vain to get a word alone with him. He had not as yet given her or Ingrid a present. Besides, there were many questions that she wanted to ask him about America. What an exciting place it must be to live! What wouldn't it mean, if she were permitted to spend only a single day in such a fairyland! Getting Master Cleng to tell about it would be the next best thing.

Finally one day when both Gunda and Mistress Catherine were taking their afternoon naps, Margit saw Master Cleng walking down the path leading to the spring and the dairy. It was usual for him to make inspection tours about the estate to see how things were going. For although Mistress Catherine insisted on managing affairs herself, Master Cleng was really interested in the place. He often gave Mistress Catherine suggestions which at the time she received indifferently. However, Margit had noticed that after he was gone Mistress Catherine did carry out many of them.

On this afternoon, Gunda had told Ingrid to keep stirring a huge pot of cheese which was simmering over the fire. Margit knew that Ingrid would not dare to leave her post for an instant for fear of letting the precious cheese scorch. This was the moment Margit had been waiting for.

She slipped out the kitchen door, leaving it slightly open, so as not to attract Ingrid's attention. She ran as fast as she could down the steep path and was soon out of sight of anyone who might chance to be looking out of one of the windows. At the bottom of the hill, she slackened her pace. Master Cleng had stopped outside the dairy. Margit held her breath. She couldn't question him in the presence of Nille, the dairymaid. But Master Cleng didn't go inside the dairy. Instead, he started walking again and disappeared behind the building. The spring flowed out of a rocky ledge there, and in hot weather Margit enjoyed drinking the fresh, cool water out of her cupped hands.

She found Master Cleng sitting on a slab of rock, sunning himself. "Master Cleng," she said a little breathlessly.

"Oh, it's you, Margit," he said. "Have you finished the work Catherine told you to do?"

"She and Gunda are having their afternoon naps," Margit said, evading his question. "Ingrid is the one Gunda told to stir the cheese today."

"It is a beautiful day for being outside," Master Cleng said smiling. He moved over to make room for Margit on the rock.

"Very beautiful," Margit murmured. Then, realizing that the moment so sought after might be lost by an unexpected interruption, she started eagerly, "Didn't you see any children in America, Master Cleng? Or young girls like me?"

He looked down at her in surprise. "Why, of course, there are small children there and young girls like you! Why do you ask?"

"Tell me, Master Cleng, what were they like?"

"America is full of fine girls and boys. Happier ones you never saw in all your life. People over there love their children very much. They want to do much for their children and they have the means to carry out their wishes. The children have beautiful parks to play in during their free time. Best of all, they are sent to school so they can grow up to become important men and women."

"Do they often get sweets—like those you have sometimes brought to Ingrid and me when you have returned home?"

Master Cleng chuckled. "That's right. I haven't given you girls your presents yet, have I?"

He drew from his pocket a flat package wrapped in brown paper. "Why don't you open it and see whether you like it," Master Cleng said.

Margit needed no second invitation. First she rolled the red string into a tiny ball and folded the paper carefully before she examined the precious thing that came out of the package. Only rarely did such a momentous event take place in her life. "Why—why, Master Cleng—it's velvet! I've never owned anything made of velvet in all my life. But—but what will I do with it?"

"Unfasten those tight braids around your head and I'll show you."

Margit's hair fell in soft curls over her shoulders. Master Cleng put his hand clumsily around the curls.

"Tie the velvet ribbon into a bow just there," he told her. "That is the style among the finest young American girls."

With trembling fingers, Margit managed to tie first a knot and then a flat bow. "But, Master Cleng, Mistress Catherine wants my hair braided and wound around my head."

Master Cleng smiled. "Perhaps it is as well that you re-braid your hair now and wind it around your head as it was before. Some day the occasion may arise when it will be all right for you to show your curls."

Margit rewrapped the package carefully and put it in the pocket of her skirt. "I didn't thank you," she said sheepishly.

"I'll consider myself thanked right now. And when you return to the house, tell Ingrid I have something for her, too. I brought a box of chocolates for the family this time, so she wouldn't have to give away her share."

Again Margit's prickly conscience bothered her. Yet that was foolish, she thought, for with whom could she share her velvet ribbon? Suddenly it came to her that she hadn't asked the questions whose answers she wanted most to hear.

"It must be wonderful for children to live in America," she said. "But how is it for those who do not have a father and mother?"

"For such children, America is the most wonderful country on earth," Master Cleng declared enthusiastically. "If, as they grow up, they are willing to work, there is no end to what they can accomplish. That is why I am helping to organize a colony which is going to migrate to America."

Margit stared wide-eyed at Master Cleng. "You—you are returning to America?" she exclaimed.

"Yes. Before long I shall be going back to arrange things for those who will be coming to establish a colony over there. I hope to make it the first Norwegian colony ever to take roots in America."

Margit's heart beat fast. "Then—then will you be living over there? Won't you ever come back?"

Master Cleng put his hand lightly on Margit's shoulder. "I hope to. Perhaps, in time, I shall be able to make Catherine, too, see that America is the land of the future."

Margit was on the verge of tears. "Then she won't be one of those who will establish the colony?"

"I'm afraid not. But my sister Carrie and her husband, Cornelius Nelson, and their children have already agreed to migrate. And Lars Larson of Stavanger, a very capable and fine man, will look after all the preparations on this side of the Atlantic."

"I wish—it's going to be terrible—we'll all miss you," Margit said brokenly.

"That's no way to talk," Master Cleng said a little brusquely, "for a young girl like you with her whole life before her. A daughter of old Viking stock, as you are, should have more spirit."

Suddenly Ingrid appeared from around the corner of the dairy. "Margit," she said, "you will have to return to the house in a hurry. Mistress Catherine and Gunda are downstairs now."

Margit jumped up. "Oh, Ingrid," she exclaimed, "Master Cleng has been telling me the most wonderful things about America and young people over there and. . . ."

"I told Gunda," Ingrid interrupted, "that you had gone down to the dairy to fetch cream for afternoon coffee." She produced a pitcher from under her apron. "If we don't return immediately, Mistress Catherine will be cross with both of us."

On their way back to the house, Margit babbled about the wonderful things Master Cleng had told her. "And do you know, Ingrid," she said, stopping and taking Ingrid by the arm, "Master Cleng will soon be going back to America. He intends to establish a colony of Norwegians there. His sister Carrie Nelson and her family will—"

Ingrid freed herself. "Can't you see Gunda standing outside the kitchen door? She's beckoning for us to hurry."

"I don't care. I wish I were going, too."

"Hush," Ingrid said, lowering her voice. "Not a word of all this either to Gunda or to Mistress Catherine. It will be bad enough when Master Cleng tells her."

From then on, Margit could think of nothing but Master Cleng's return to America, and the date set for his departure seemed to arrive unbelievably soon.

Mistress Catherine and Ingrid and Margit were packing his knapsack with provisions to last him during the crossing of the Atlantic. They wrapped flat bread and cheese and dried meat in clean cloths, and filled a small wooden container with butter. There was another container for sugar, one for salt and one for coffee. As Margit worked, she had all she could do to keep back the tears.

Just as they had finished the packing, Carrie Nelson and Cornelius with their children and Master Cleng's father and brother came to say good-by.

"We'll be seeing you over there before long, Brother Cleng," Carrie Nelson said, beaming. "Be sure to select land for us that is the very best to be had."

"On that you can depend," Master Cleng assured her. "And I'll arrange for our farms to lie side by side."

"The children talk of nothing else but of going to America," Carrie Nelson said. "Even though Cornelius and I might want to change our plans about migrating, we simply couldn't disappoint them."

"You mustn't do that," Master Cleng said quickly. "I'm counting on you and Cornelius to be the stalwarts of the group. And," he added with a gleam in his eye, "consider the great loss the American nation would suffer if you failed to put in your appearance over there." He turned to his father. "You ought to join us in America, too."

The father shook his head. "No, son," he said. "Such adventure is for younger ones."

Margit's heart went out to the bearded, white-haired old man. She had noticed during the serving of coffee how his eyes followed Master Cleng's every movement.

"And you?" Master Cleng said, looking inquiringly at his brother.

"I couldn't leave Father. I'll be the only one he has left in Norway after you and Carrie are gone."

"Your brother is a good son," Mistress Catherine said, glancing sharply at Master Cleng.

"Well, if any of you change your minds and decide to

come over," Master Cleng said, "I'll do all I can to help you. And, Father, I want you to know that you would be cared for in America just as well as you would in Norway."

"Idle promises are easily given and easily broken," Mistress Catherine said sourly.

Master Cleng looked hard at her for a moment and then turned away.

She is certainly doing all she can to make things hard for him before he goes, Margit thought.

When it came time for the actual leave-taking the family clustered around Master Cleng outside the house. They were joined by the cottagers and the servants. Master Cleng shook hands with each one and had a kind word for each. When it came time for Margit to say good-by, she smiled and told him, "Good luck in America, Master Cleng."

He smiled in return and said, "Good luck in Norway. And the next time we meet, be prepared for some even more exciting details about the great Wonderland."

Cornelius Nelson was to go to the landing where Master Cleng would board a boat to take him to the city of Stavanger. He strapped his knapsack on his back and the two started off on foot.

For a few minutes the group stood watching them as they made their way down the hill. Then Mistress Catherine said, "The wind is chilly, and there is work to be done."

The day following Master Cleng's departure, Mistress Catherine sent for Margit to come into the parlor.

"I want you to go up to the weaving room," Mistress Catherine said. "There is a pile of clothes there which need patching and darning. Ingrid will work with Gunda down in the kitchen until you have finished."

Margit went upstairs obediently. There were worn socks, two shirts, two pairs of trousers and a knitted scarf. All of them belonged to Master Cleng. After Margit had finished the mending, Mistress Catherine came into the weaving room. She had several handkerchiefs, a walking stick, a box of pictures, and a notebook in which he had written observations about his travels.

"No one here will have use for these things," Mistress Catherine said, "so I am sending them to my brother's home." She began putting one thing after another into a ragged cloth sack. She picked up the notebook that had dropped to the floor. "No one at my brother's will be interested in this scribbling. Here, Margit, take it. Tell Gunda to use it for kindling on the hearth."

Margit felt her cheeks burn with anger. What right had Mistress Catherine to dispose of Master Cleng's personal belongings in this highhanded manner? Suppose he saw fit to return some day, what then?

After Mistress Catherine had gone downstairs, Margit opened the notebook and began to examine it. In neat, closely written pages, Master Cleng had recorded observations he had made in various countries he had visited: Germany, France, Belgium, Denmark, Sweden and England. Halfway through the book, she came across the caption *America*. Margit quickly glanced over page after page. There were notations about people, cities, prices of food and clothing. There were lists of varieties of trees and flowers, classes of animals and birds and types of soil and crops suitable to be cultivated there. On one page she read, "America is like the Atlantic Ocean, in that you can spread out your arms and breathe freely." Farther on, Master Cleng had written, "It's good to have gotten away from the eternal shadows of the Norwegian mountains." Then, as if he had suffered from a momentary sense of guilt because of disloyalty to his native land, he had scribbled, "There's really nothing the matter with Norway. It is a wonderful country. It is only because people in authority misuse their trust and shut out the light from the average man that conditions over there are presently difficult. Some day the lamp of American liberty may shed its light across the sea and bring light and good fortune to my people over there."

"Margit, what are you doing up in the weaving room so long?" Mistress Catherine called sternly.

Margit closed the notebook. "I'm just finishing," she said. "I am coming right now."

But before she did, she walked softly into her bedroom. She opened the door of the cupboard and slipped the notebook under her box of treasures on the top shelf. To ensure greater safety, she took a wool scarf that hung on a peg, folded it and laid it carefully on top of her treasure box, completely covering it and the notebook. She hoped that hidden as the notebook was now, no one would find it, particularly Mistress Catherine. For at some time in the future, she intended to see that the notebook was sent to Master Cleng over in America.

CHAPTER THREE

The weeks after Master Cleng's departure dragged end-lessly for Ingrid and Margit. Mistress Catherine was more exacting than ever and neither of the girls was able to suit her, no matter how careful they tried to be with the work. Mistress Catherine was cross with Gunda, too, and Gunda in turn took out her hurt feelings on the two girls. The weather was gloomy and rain poured in torrents unceasingly out of low, dark gray clouds.

"There isn't one bright thing about this place," Ingrid complained to Margit one especially trying day in Novem-ber. "If I couldn't go home every night to my father and mother and two brothers, I couldn't stand it here."

"Now you know how life is for me," Margit said. "I feel as though I'm in prison, working in this dreary kitchen, day in and day out. If only Mistress Catherine would allow us to light a candle these short dark days, things might not be quite so bad. But no, there must be no wasting of tallow, in spite of the fact that this virtue of hers may cost us our eyesight."

Ingrid burst into hearty laughter.

At that moment, Mistress Catherine appeared in the hall

doorway. "Time," she said, looking disapprovingly at Ingrid, "is a valuable possession. See that neither of you laughs it away."

All the while, Master Cleng's notebook lay safely hidden under Margit's box of treasures, but it was a constant source of worry to her. Any day, Mistress Catherine might make one of her periodic tours of inspection, when not even the most trifling detail escaped her keen eye. In her present bad mood, she would be even more alert to find anything unusual or displeasing to her. If she discovered the notebook, which she would not fail to do, she would personally and without delay supervise the destruction of its every leaf. In addition, she would inflict some severe punishment upon Margit for her disobedience, and life would be more unbearable than ever.

January brought extreme cold and mounds of snow. For several days Ingrid was unable to get from her parents' house to Mistress Catherine's. None of the other servants or cottagers put in their appearance, either. That is, none but Gunda, of course. Margit found herself confined in a shrunken world, inhabited by only three uncongenial and unhappy human beings—Mistress Catherine, Gunda and herself. Ingrid's return marked an exciting event in this desolation.

By February, no word had yet been received from Master Cleng.

Then one morning, the sun rose into a clear blue sky. The kitchen was so bright that Margit was able to bone the fish for breakfast without having to go over to the window. Gunda went about her work with less of a limp and Mistress Catherine, for once, found no fault with the food that was served her. Ingrid arrived out of breath as though she had been running. There was a glint of excitement in her eye and a broad smile on her lips. To Margit, it was as though some great and good power had suddenly brought new life and light into her drab world.

With her back turned toward Gunda and Mistress Catherine, Ingrid faced Margit and moved her lips without making any sound. Twice she did this, and the second time, Margit made out the words, "I have something to tell you." Margit was consumed with curiosity, but she knew better than to try to question Ingrid then. Finally Mistress Catherine went into the parlor and Gunda put a shawl over her head and shoulders, picked up a pail and left for the dairy.

When the two girls were alone in the kitchen, Margit said, "I've had a feeling ever since I woke up this morning that something exciting has happened. Quick, before Gunda gets back, out with your secret."

"There's been a letter from Master Cleng." Ingrid spoke in a low voice and looked toward the door leading into the hall. Mistress Catherine often appeared there at the most unexpected moments.

"Who got it? What did he say?"

"His brother and his father, though he sent greetings to us all."

"But what did he say?" Margit persisted.

"He has bought land for himself and for Carrie Nelson in America. Carrie was the one who told Mother about the letter. Mother said Carrie is simply wild with joy."

"When will Carrie and Cornelius and the children be leaving Tysvaer?" Margit asked.

"She wasn't sure. But Master Cleng wants them and the others who intend to join the colony to come as soon as possible."

The door from the outside opened. Gunda was back with a pail of milk in one hand and a leg of dried goat meat in the other. Margit and Ingrid concentrated on the dishes they were washing.

From the news of the letter, Margit realized that now it was more important than ever for Master Cleng to have his travel notebook, since it contained so much useful information about America. It had taken him three years at least to gather these notes, and he would be needing them now.

That same afternoon, Gunda sent Ingrid and Margit down to the washhouse to finish some mangling left over from the first spring clothes washing. As soon as the work got under way, Margit confided to Ingrid her problem about the notebook. Ingrid was as much concerned as Margit.

"You'll have to do something right away," Ingrid advised her. "Once this washing is done, Mistress Catherine is going to be poking into every corner of every building on the place before she finishes."

"But what can I do with it?" Margit asked.

"You'll have to think of something. At least don't keep it in the cupboard. Mistress Catherine simply loves to go through such places."

"Since Carrie Nelson is going, the easiest thing would be to send the notebook with her," Margit said. "She thinks the world of her brother and, if I stressed how important it is that Master Cleng receive it, she would consent to get it safely into his hands. But, without meaning to, she might mention it to Mistress Catherine, even though I cautioned her not to."

"I guess you're right, Margit. Carrie Nelson is so good and so unsuspecting that she wouldn't understand Mistress Catherine's having anything against Master Cleng's receiving it, not even after all the jolts Mistress Catherine has given her in the past."

"The first time Master Cleng told me about the colony,

he said that Lars Larson was going to look after all the preparations here in Norway. Perhaps I could get the notebook
to him, Ingrid."

"That would be almost as difficult to manage as crossing
the Atlantic Ocean," Ingrid laughed. "It takes a long day's
hard pulling to row a boat from the island here over to the
city of Stavanger. You couldn't start out alone and, besides,
where would you get the boat?"

That night, Margit took the notebook to bed with her.
Perhaps, during the day, she could leave it under her pillow
or the mattress. But no, Mistress Catherine was as eagle-eyed
about beds as she was about cupboards. For hours, Margit
lay awake thinking. Any number of hiding places occurred
to her: the cedar chest where extra bedding was kept; inside
the big clock in the front hall; under the workbench in the
kitchen; and in the washhouse, the dairy, the harness and
shoemaker shop; the carpenter shop; the meat and fish smoke-
house; even the barns. But she knew none of them would do.
When dawn broke Margit had reached a temporary but
wholly unsatisfactory solution to her problem. She would,
as she had done now, take the notebook to bed with her at
night. Each morning she would conceal it in the deep pocket
of her voluminous skirt. There were two drawbacks to this
solution. She might forget some morning to remove the notebook from under her pillow, particularly if she were in a
hurry or distracted in some way. Or, with a sudden motion
while bending over, the notebook might slip out of her
pocket. But she'd have to risk either contingency. On Sundays she'd have to slip it inside the bosom of her best dress.

One day when Ingrid and Margit were alone in the kitchen,
Ingrid said, "Mother mentioned last night that Lars Larson
is looking for a girl to help his wife get ready for the journey
to America. She expects her baby in the fall, and it is already

hard for her to get her work done. Mother said they will pay
well too. Carrie Nelson told her so."

Margit felt her heart beat faster. "Why don't you go, Ingrid? You have often said that your parents think Mistress
Catherine pays you entirely too little." And, Margit thought,
if you do, I'll get you to take Master Cleng's notebook to
Lars Larson.

"No," Ingrid said promptly. "I couldn't stay away from
home that long. I'd miss my family too much. Besides, it
would mean only a temporary job, and I doubt that Mistress
Catherine would take me back afterward."

"Maybe she would, Ingrid. She'd never get anyone else to
work the way you do."

"No, I couldn't risk it. Mother said that too. But why don't
you go? It would give you a chance to deliver the notebook
to Lars Larson yourself."

"I'd be worse off than you. You could at least live with
your parents if Mistress Catherine refused to take you back.
I'd have no place to go. And Mistress Catherine would be
more furious with me, I'm sure, than she would ever be with
you."

"I guess maybe you're right," Ingrid agreed. "Yet it does
seem a pity. By the way, where have you been keeping the
notebook since I spoke to you about it?"

Margit told her.

"You're taking an awful chance. Do you know that yesterday, when you bent over to get a pan from under the
workbench, I noticed something sticking out of your pocket?
I was going to speak to you about it, but Mistress Catherine
came in just then and I forgot. Suppose, at that very moment,
the notebook had slipped entirely out of the pocket? You'd
have been in a very bad spot."

That night Margit did not sleep at all. The more she

thought about her conversation with Ingrid, the more she realized that she could not leave matters to chance. She would have to map out a course of action. And she would have to be even more watchful about keeping the notebook out of Mistress Catherine's sight in the meantime.

She solved the second problem as soon as dawn broke. She removed the precious notebook from under her pillow and, with care, ripped off its slightly stiff covers. Then, turning the pocket of her everyday dress inside out, she stitched the notebook to the very bottom of the pocket. She sighed with relief as she hung the dress back on the chair. Now she could concentrate on finding a solution to her first problem.

While she worked, Margit considered various people whom she might ask to do her errand for her: the servants on the estate; the cottagers and members of their families; other people in the parish. For one reason or another, she discounted them all. Then the proverb of being well served by serving oneself entered her mind. She should have followed Ingrid's suggestion in the first place. Whatever the consequences might be, she knew now that she would have to go to Stavanger herself.

To ask Mistress Catherine's permission would be useless. In the first place, she would have to give the reason for wanting to go and that would mean admitting that she had been disobedient in not having destroyed the notebook. After such an admission all hope would be lost. If she openly defied Mistress Catherine and told her that she intended to leave anyway, Mistress Catherine would find means of preventing this. The only course Margit could follow was to slip away without Mistress Catherine's permission or knowledge. She would rather not do this, but there seemed to be no other way.

After Margit thought she had solved this problem to her satisfaction, others began to present themselves to her. It would take time to get down to the landing where the boats were moored. It would take more time to secure a boat, if she could manage this at all. Then there was the wide expanse of water to be covered. She knew nothing about sailing and was not too skillful with oars. It might prove as baffling to try to find a boatman willing to take her across to Stavanger. And should she succeed in overcoming all these difficulties, Mistress Catherine would be sure to send someone after her. Margit shuddered to think of her future in Mistress Catherine's kitchen if she were overtaken. But, in any event, after the Larsons had sailed, she would be left alone on the streets of Stavanger without a roof over her head.

She would just have to let Mistress Catherine know she intended to go to Stavanger. There was no other way. But she would make no mention of the notebook. She would simply tell her that she had heard that Martha Larson needed a girl to help her and that she wanted the job. It took Margit one whole night to come to this decision.

The following morning, immediately after breakfast, Margit went into the parlor. Mistress Catherine sat by a small table. Her immense black leather Bible, with its gold clasp and trimmings, was open before her. As Margit entered the room, Mistress Catherine looked up from her reading.

"Mistress Catherine," Margit said, doing her best to appear calm, "I would like to ask you something."

"Morning hours have gold in their mouths," Mistress Catherine said crisply. "Whatever you have to say must wait until later. You see that I am occupied, and, as for yourself, there is work in the kitchen that has to be done."

Margit's heart sank, but she did not dare argue. What if she never got the chance to present her plan to Mistress Catherine?

That night Mistress Catherine complained of rheumatism,

and told Margit to rub her back and neck with Jacob's oil.

As soon as Mistress Catherine was lying in her bed, swathed in woolen cloths, Margit decided to speak.

"Mistress Catherine," she said, "Martha Larson wants a girl to help her get ready to sail for America, and I want to go there and work for her."

If Margit had fired off a shot from a gun, Mistress Catherine could not have been more surprised. She sat up in bed and stared at Margit, dumfounded.

"Martha expects a baby in the fall," Margit went on, gaining courage as she talked. "She needs someone, because it is hard for her to get her work done."

"And what do you think is to become of me?" Mistress Catherine snapped. "I might have known. Ingratitude is the way of the world."

Oh, dear me, Margit thought. If I don't stop her from going off on this tangent, I'm lost. Suddenly she was seized with what seemed like a saving inspiration. "You don't understand," Margit said aloud. "I *am* grateful. And to show you how much I appreciate all you have done for me, I promise to give you every *krone* Martha Larson pays me. Ingrid's mother was the one who heard about the job, and she said the Larsons will pay well."

The stern look on Mistress Catherine's face gave way to a more relaxed expression. "Well," she said, "I could make use of the money. You have been a great expense to me all these years. If Gunda can arrange that you get some of your work done before you leave, I may be able to manage without you for a few weeks."

Gunda consented grudgingly, and Mistress Catherine agreed to stand by her promise. Margit was more than relieved. With this seemingly insurmountable obstacle removed, she was ready to brave anything. For she would be free now to carry out her project, which had become almost an obsession with her.

For weeks, Margit worked with more enthusiasm than she had ever shown before. Under ordinary circumstances, she would have felt she was being driven. Mistress Catherine had always demanded a full day's work from everyone in her household. But now she begrudged Margit even a moment's inactivity during her waking hours. She thought of all sorts of odd jobs, which Margit considered unnecessary, but did uncomplainingly: rewinding balls of yarn in Mistress Catherine's knitting bag; repotting and changing the soil of all her house plants; going over bed and table linen in her cedar chests and counting every piece; and rearranging spools of thread in her sewing basket, according to the size of the spool and the color of the thread.

Ingrid and Gunda, too, were caught up in the whirl of scrubbing and cooking and baking demanded by Mistress Catherine. Margit's conscience bothered her to think that they both were being imposed upon because of her. To make it up to them, she decided to give Gunda her silver bell. And, much as it hurt to part with the blue velvet ribbon, she would add that to the silk kerchief for Ingrid.

Then one evening, Mistress Catherine called Margit into her bedroom.

"Ingrid's brother is going to Stavanger in a few days. I mean to have him take some sheep and a pig that we have just butchered to market. There will be room for you in the boat, too."

"Oh, thank you!" Margit exclaimed in spite of her resolution not to sound too eager.

"But mind you," Mistress Catherine warned, "you are to bring me all the wages the Larsons pay you. Not a single *ore* is to be spent on foolishness."

Anger surged up and Margit bit her lip, determined this time to control her emotions.

"Now leave me," Mistress Catherine said fretfully. "I feel pains all through my body. I don't know why I have to be a martyr for the convenience of others."

The night before Margit was to leave, Mistress Catherine supervised her packing: one nightgown, a change of underwear and an apron.

"Since you are going away to work," Mistress Catherine said, "I am not sending your Sunday dress."

"But traveling so far and—"

"Your everyday dress will be good enough to wear in a boat which you will be sharing with dead sheep and a pig," Mistress Catherine snapped.

Margit blinked back the tears. She had pictured herself making rather a good appearance dressed in her best when she presented herself to city folk like the Larsons at Stavanger. But she did not dare to argue for fear that, at the last minute, she might be forbidden to leave at all.

However, after Mistress Catherine had gone into her own room and closed the door, Margit reached up and took down her box of treasures, opened her travel bundle and tucked it inside. She would take her treasures along for safekeeping. She could picture Ingrid's pleasure and even Gunda's when they received these gifts on her return.

Margit sat down on the chair near the window and gazed out into the gathering spring twilight. But actually she saw nothing out there. Her mind was too full of pictures of what she would be seeing in only a few hours: the city of Stavanger; strange houses; hundreds of new people. Even the boat ride from the island of Tysvaer, where she had always lived, over to the mainland on which Stavanger was situated would be an entirely new and exciting experience. She would be spending a whole day on the water.

She hoped she could sleep away the hours between now and morning. If she had to lie awake, the suspense would be unendurable. But it really didn't matter how she spent the night. Tomorrow morning she would be starting out on the greatest and most wonderful adventure of her entire life, and she intended to make the most of every minute.

CHAPTER FOUR

If Margit had been suddenly brought to a different planet, her life could not have changed more than it did when she started to work for the Larsons. Martha was young and pretty, with the friendliness of an elder sister. Somehow, Margit had not expected to find such an attractive person working in a kitchen—even though it was her own. Margit had always thought that only princesses or queens or important personages in society could be so charming.

Since Margit was to be a servant in the household of the Larsons, she had, on her arrival, gone to the kitchen door. But Martha Larson had immediately piloted her into the parlor and invited her to sit down.

"How kind of Mistress Catherine to send you to help me," she told Margit. "Now I know how foolish I was to worry about it. God always supplies us with whatever we need when we need it most."

Martha Larson's instructions were so explicit, yet so kindly and considerate, that from the very first morning Margit was able to take over her duties with confidence. She even looked forward with eager anticipation to attacking each new task, in order to show Martha Larson that she was capable of performing it.

Every morning she placed a snow-white linen napkin on the shining silver tray and set on it lump sugar, cream, two cups and saucers, a small plate of tiny cakes and a pot of coffee and brought it into the Larsons' bedroom. Then she went back to the kitchen to prepare breakfast. This consisted of thinly sliced dark oven bread, cold or creamed fish, cheese and milk. After breakfast had been served and the dishes washed, she washed and peeled the vegetables—usually potatoes, carrots or onions—for the large noon meal. Martha Larson taught her new ways of cooking fish and meat. And there seemed to be no end to the varieties of delicious soups and puddings that Martha Larson knew how to make. Margit enjoyed both getting the food ready and eating it, for to her each meal was a fine feast. To be sure, there were times when the dishes Martha asked Margit to prepare failed to turn out as expected. But Martha only laughed good-naturedly and said that every cook was entitled to a few mistakes, especially if she was under sixteen years of age.

After noon, Margit scoured the tin prongs of the wooden-handled forks and the blades of the knives with fine, white, damp sand. She also rubbed the copper coffee kettle and pots and pans with vinegar and salt so they shone and she could see a reflection of herself in them. The kitchen was even brighter in the afternoon than during the morning and a gentle breeze blew in through the open windows the sweet scent of flowers and newly cut grass.

At home in Mistress Catherine's kitchen, Margit had detested any job that meant working with fish. She had also inwardly rebelled against the eternal scouring and scrubbing that was demanded of her. Yet, strangely enough, she actually enjoyed performing these very same tasks either with Martha herself or with Lars Larson's deaf-and-dumb sister Sarah.

In some matters, Martha Larson was more particular than

Mistress Catherine had been. She insisted upon certain niceties in serving every meal, whether there happened to be guests present or not. And clothes and bedding were hung out to air in the sunshine at least once a week.

One of the new experiences Margit especially enjoyed was watching the people who walked by on the street. The Larson home was situated on a corner, so that Margit could look out from both the parlor and the kitchen windows. She grew to recognize some of the passers-by who often came that way: an old man pulling a wagon in which a little girl sat with a puppy in her lap; the young couple, always walking arm in arm; and the young boy leading the sweet old lady by the hand. Who were they and what were their lives like? Margit would have liked to have gone out to talk to them and to question them, but she contented herself with making up stories about them for her own amusement.

The most thrilling and challenging job Martha Larson assigned to her and the one in which she took the greatest pride was going to the store to do the family shopping. At Mistress Catherine's, almost all the food was produced right on the place. The wool for the clothes was sheared from the sheep. Hides from the cattle were dried and tanned and came out as shoes from Hans's shoemaker and harness shop on the estate. On rare occasions Mistress Catherine took mysterious trips from which she returned with salt and pepper and spices and other necessities which could not be produced at home. But no one was ever permitted to accompany her. No one was ever taken into her confidence concerning these transactions.

Up to the time Margit entered the employ of the Larsons, she had never handled money. She knew there was such a commodity, for she had seen Mistress Catherine count it—paper bills and round, metal coins—whenever she was paid for cows or pigs or sheep or anything else she had to sell. She also learned that one hundred *ore* equaled a *krone*, but that was all.

Now Martha Larson entrusted her with both *ore* and *kroner*. The first time Margit went to the store, she was so intrigued by all the wonderful things on display that she almost forgot what she was supposed to buy. Now she remembered that Mistress Catherine had mentioned such places after returning from her mysterious trips. But Margit also remembered that Mistress Catherine had often said that anyone who frequented them too often was destined to utter ruin. Yet Martha Larson sent Margit to this store almost daily, and to all appearances, the Larsons seemed both prosperous and very happy.

It might have been expected that Martha would have become impatient with Margit, having to teach her so many things in such a short time. Instead, she never once spoke with aggravation, and after Margit had been in Stavanger only a short while Martha said to her one day, "My husband is so relieved that you are here with me and doing so much to help me. Now he can go about his business in the city, attending to all the necessary details preparatory to our sailing. I have told him how very dependable you are."

This praise was wonderful for Margit to hear. From the very first time she had met Lars Larson, she had been greatly impressed and, as time went on, she regarded him more and more highly. Small in stature, dark-haired and brown-eyed, with no distinguishing features, in a crowd he would probably not have been singled out from many others. But as soon as he spoke, there was a certain air of power and authority about him that even his sweet smile and gentle manner did not conceal. Margit had noticed, too, that all the people who came to the house seemed to have a very high opinion of him and deferred to his judgment.

One evening, Martha Larson said to Margit, "A few of our friends will be here tonight for a meeting. Would you like to join us?"

Margit was pleased. She did not know the nature of the gathering, but she accepted eagerly. Every new experience was to be cherished.

At about seven o'clock both men and women began to arrive. As she opened the door for them, Margit was surprised to see that the women wore gray wool dresses, with very full skirts and white fichus at the neck, exactly like those worn by Martha Larson and Lars's sister Sarah. And on their heads were wide, strange-looking bonnets. After they had been ushered into the parlor, everyone sat with bowed heads and folded hands. There was complete silence in the room. Margit waited expectantly for something to happen.

Then, one after another, women as well as men began to speak. They told of their love of God and of the great love which God had for them. They seemed to speak spontaneously, pouring out their declarations of faith without any attempt to make them sound elegant or dramatic. Margit sat listening to this strange religious service with mixed feelings. She was both curious and a little frightened. Mistress Catherine had been so strict in her teachings and so positive that she was right that to witness this unusual approach to religion was both exciting and unsettling.

But there was such humility and sincerity among those giving their testimonials that Margit was reassured. Surely there could be nothing wrong in the attitude of these earnest people toward their Saviour. Lars Larson, especially, spoke so lovingly about the Master and of what He meant to him and his family, that Margit's heart went out to him. He was most certainly a very good man. And she was convinced now that he could be trusted to deliver Master Cleng's travel notebook to him. She would ask him at her earliest opportunity and get him to promise to do it. This would take a load off her mind, since she would have accomplished what she had set out to do in coming to Stavanger.

But during the days which followed, no opportunity offered itself to broach the subject to Lars Larson. Martha was in the midst of preparing for the sailing, and Lars Larson, himself, was gone from dawn to dark, getting the boat and the stores ready. Margit's job was to help Martha as much as she possibly could.

"I'm faced with two great problems," Martha told Margit. "What can I take along and what must I dispose of. Cleng Peerson has written my husband saying that it is lawful to sell only a very small boat in an American port. So my husband has warned me that I must limit our baggage to absolute necessities. He has taken over a very small vessel, renaming it the *Restoration*. It is now being overhauled to make it fit for ocean travel. With so little space, strict regulations must be followed. We shall be allowed only one chest to hold provisions. Anything else must, of necessity, be carefully screened."

Martha Larson had been given a cedar chest at the time of her marriage, and she decided this would do to hold the food. Margit helped her pack the chest. At the very bottom were bins for meal, coffee, tea, salt, dried legs of goat and mutton, and salted and dried fish. Above the bins were shelves on which were placed wooden containers with tight covers to hold butter and cheese and as much flat bread as could possibly be packed into the rest of the space.

"Now there is the bedding to be taken care of," Martha said, when the chest had finally been closed and locked. "My husband says there will be almost no space for berths. People will have to sleep in hammocks, on the floor of the cabin and anywhere else there is space enough for a person to lie stretched out at full length. Because of my condition, we must have a berth. But the amount of bedding we allow ourselves must be extremely limited." Martha finally decided on three white wool-lined sheep pelts, one for each member of her family.

When it came to clothing for the voyage, Martha was even more distressed. "Lars says that the forecastle under the deck will have to be reserved for the seven men of the crew. This means that we shall have only the hold under the back part of the deck for storage. In addition to the chests of provisions, which cannot be crowded into the center of the boat, there will have to be tanks for fresh water and iron for ballast down in the hold. So I guess we'll just have to go on wearing what we start out with on our backs. Sarah and I will put on our best dresses, and my husband his good suit. We'll all sleep in our underwear. I do hope that we'll be able to manage airing our outer clothing once in a while during the night."

"How long will it take to cross the Atlantic?" Margit asked.

"Lars says we must be prepared for weeks, even months," Martha Larson sighed. "Because of this, I shall insist on a fairly good supply of clothes for the baby, in case it is born before we reach America."

"But wouldn't that be—be—terrible?" Margit asked, completely taken aback at such a possibility.

"Difficult perhaps, but not terrible," Martha said. "But now we must begin dismantling the house. I have left that for the last. We'll keep the most necessary things as long as we can."

This remark made Margit realize that her stay with the

Larsons was nearing an end. Still she had found no favorable time for discussing Master Cleng's notebook with Lars Larson. He was gone from morning till night, coming home only to sleep and often that was for only a few hours. If she didn't give him the travel notebook very soon, her whole trip to Stavanger might easily turn out to be pointless. One after another, the Larsons' treasures were either sold or given away —the lovely dining room table and chairs, dishes, silver, the fine cupboard, the beautifully carved chest which Lars Larson had made himself for his bride.

Every day, the house took on a more and more barren and desolate appearance.

"I'm going to give all my cooking utensils to the Elias Tastads," Martha told Margit. "They have had so much ill luck lately."

"Won't you be able to take any of them on the voyage?" Margit asked.

"Yes. Lars says each family will need a kettle for cooking porridge, fish and anything else we housewives can concoct from our limited supplies. We'll take our coffee kettle along, too." Martha chuckled. "A Norwegian housewife couldn't attempt even a semblance of housekeeping without that."

When it came to the pictures on the wall, Martha disposed of all but one without a murmur. The exception was the oil painting of her home farm on the Island of Tysvaer.

"Father gave it to me when I left home," Martha said with tears in her eyes. "I simply cannot leave it behind."

Margit had a bright idea. "Why don't you cut the canvas out of the frame and roll it up?"

Martha pondered for a moment. "That would make it easier to take along. But suppose the painting got spoiled rolled up that way?"

"Couldn't you place it on the inner side of your bunk?" Margit suggested.

Martha looked dubious.

Margit glanced around the room, taking in the few things that were left. "What about this bolt of cloth you said Sarah just finished weaving? Couldn't we wind it around the frame and all, and tie paper outside the cloth? It would take up almost no space, set up against the wall behind the baggage in the hold."

"I'll ask Lars," Martha said. "If he thinks it is at all fair to the others, he will allow me to take it along."

In a corner of the parlor, the cradle was still standing. "Lars made it as soon as we learned we were to have a child," Martha Larson said, regarding it tenderly. "That was long before we had really made up our minds to migrate to America."

"Couldn't you have one of the smaller children sleep in it until the baby comes?" Margit asked.

Martha shook her head. "No. I want the cradle and the baby's things new and fresh for its arrival."

"Then why don't you tell your husband that if he hangs the cradle up against the ceiling in the lower part of the boat, it won't take up any extra space?"

Martha beamed. "I declare, Margit, you have more imagination than anyone I know. You ought to be sailing for America yourself!"

As the two packed the baby's things into the cradle, Margit felt a flush of warmth and pleasure at the compliment Martha had given her. She had been so used to obeying unquestioningly the orders of both Mistress Catherine and Gunda that, up to now, there had been few occasions when she had been allowed to do any thinking of her own.

"Well, I guess that just about finishes everything," Martha said. "I've left out my husband's good suit and Sarah's and my best dresses, and fresh underwear to put on the morning before we board the ship. I'll take them along when Sarah and I go over to the Tastads this afternoon. We'll be staying there over night. And after you and Lars have brought the baggage down to the *Restoration*, he will be coming directly over to the Tastads."

"Don't you worry at all about things down in the boat," Margit said. "I'll help your husband with everything that needs to be done there."

"Are you sure you won't mind coming back to the empty house?" Martha Larson asked a little anxiously.

"Of course, I won't mind. I'll find the key hanging in the entry, go inside and take my bundle of clothes and leave right away to meet Ingrid's brother at the store. He will be sure to be there. We got word through Carrie Nelson that he would be taking them to Stavanger and would bring me back to Tysvaer with him when he returned."

"And you have the money, Margit?"

"Oh yes, I have it tied in the piece of cloth you gave me and that is pinned securely inside my dress."

At that moment, Lars Larson arrived and he and Margit set out immediately for the pier where the *Restoration* was moored. There was a great hubbub on board. People were rushing to and fro, trying to find places for the luggage they were taking along. Margit helped Lars Larson carry the cradle and the chest on board, and then they went back to the wagon for the oil painting and the two kettles. It took considerable calculation before Lars Larson found a place where he felt the oil painting would not deprive anyone else of needed space. Finally he slid it behind some luggage at the very back of the hold. He placed the kettles on top of their food chest.

"But the bedding," Margit exclaimed suddenly.

"I brought that down late last night. It's in our bunk," Lars Larson told her.

When Margit started for the *Restoration* with Lars Larson, she had two things in mind. She wanted to help with the luggage and so relieve Martha Larson of any heavy lifting. After everything had been placed on board and she and Lars Larson were about to part, she would take out the precious travel notebook and ask him to deliver it in person to Master Cleng when he arrived in America.

But as soon as she stepped on board the *Restoration*, she became intensely interested in the ship itself. It was so much larger than any she had ever seen and there were so many intriguing things to examine. It was really two stories high for there was a narrow ladder that led down to the cabin. Then there was the forecastle for the crew and the hold in the stern where much of the luggage and the water tanks and other things were kept. But what excited her most were the steering wheel, where the captain would direct the vessel, the compass which would tell him he was on his course, and the dory on the foredeck, which, Lars Larson explained, would be used in case of emergency.

The passengers who were to board the vessel in the morning were certainly fortunate. It would be wonderful to sail across the Atlantic Ocean in that fine boat! And most wonderful of all to land in America where Master Cleng would be on the pier ready to welcome them.

As Margit worked with Lars Larson, she grew more and more envious of those who were about to migrate. If only there were a way for her to go, too.

One more passenger wouldn't really matter, especially if she had no luggage. But it was too late now to get permission from anyone.

Margit's eyes traveled toward the dory. It was turned upside down with just enough space between its upper edge and the deck—yes, by sliding on her back, she could make it.

The thought at first was frightening. But why not? It would be her one chance. If she didn't, Ingrid's brother would row her back to Tysvaer to slave in Mistress Catherine's kitchen for the rest of her life.

But suppose she should fail—suppose someone discovered her before the *Restoration* sailed, what then? If she sought employment in Stavanger, Mistress Catherine would be sure to find out and send for her. Margit shuddered to think of what would happen after that. Her life then would be even worse than poor Gunda's.

But nothing ventured, nothing gained. The risk would be more than worth while in consideration of the reward if she should succeed.

Just before she left the *Restoration*, Margit took one last look around. It would be dark when she returned tonight and she would have to be sure of every step she took.

CHAPTER FIVE

Back in Lars Larson's house, Margit found the key on the peg in the entry and opened the door to the kitchen. Without the presence of the Larsons and barren of their possessions, the house seemed a strange place. She went from empty room to empty room. It was as though she were taking a last look at something she was leaving behind forever. For, if she brought to fruition the idea that had suddenly taken root in her mind just before she left the *Restoration*, she would, in all likelihood, never see the inside of a Norwegian home for the rest of her life. The idea was a daring one and at times the very thought of carrying it out frightened her almost out of her wits. Still, it was now or never. The thought of what the success of her plan might mean to her future was so far beyond anything she had ever hoped for that she would simply have to take the chance. But before she took the final step, her conscience dictated something which she must do first.

Her traveling bundle was on the wide window ledge in the dining room, where she had left it. She picked it up and, going to a dark corner in the hall where she would not be seen from the street, she sat down on the floor. Carefully she

opened the bundle. There was her nightgown and her underwear, her treasures, some pieces of paper and a pencil which
Martha Larson had given her. With utmost care, she wrote
Gunda's name and wrapped it around the bell. On another
piece she wrote Ingrid's name and in it she wrapped the kerchief and the beautiful blue velvet ribbon. Now that she
might be mingling with American girls her own age, it would
have been nice to have dressed her hair like theirs. But Ingrid
deserved both gifts and much more. Then she took the bundle
containing her money from inside her dress, wrote Mistress
Catherine's name on her last piece of paper and pinned it
securely on the bundle, so that there would be no mistake that
she had kept her promise to give her all her wages. She would
leave word at the store where she and Ingrid's brother were
to meet that he was to tell Ingrid to take out something which
was hers before she delivered the bundle to Mistress Catherine.
After all this was finished, Margit tied up the bundle even
more carefully than before.

She would have to hurry to get to the store ahead of Ingrid's brother. She knew how much he loved to walk around
in the streets of Stavanger so that he would have interesting
things to tell the family at home. But since this time he was
to take her back to Mistress Catherine's place, he might feel
duty bound to curtail his curiosity and leave earlier than usual.
Fortunately he was not at the store when Margit arrived,
and the storekeeper promised faithfully to deliver the bundle
and the message. Margit thanked the storekeeper for his kindness and left.

It was too early to start for the pier where the *Restoration*
was tied. She could not risk returning to the Larsons' house
for fear Ingrid's brother might go there in search of her. It
seemed she had roamed about for hours before the endless
summer daylight finally gave way to a slowly gathering twi-

light. Her feet ached and her throat was dry. Her gray wool dress was damp with perspiration brought out by nervousness and the heat. She decided to start making her way down toward the water front, since she did not know what time it was and nights in early July were so short that dawn might come without warning.

As Margit made her way over the cobblestone streets, she rehearsed in her mind how she would go about boarding the *Restoration*. Her first concern would have to be to locate the right pier where the boat was moored. She ought to be able to do that without difficulty, since she had a good land-mark to go by. When she and Lars Larson got into the wagon at the end of the pier that afternoon, she had noticed a high pile of brand-new lumber. The wood was very light and should, therefore, be easily seen even in the dark.

She would get through the shed between the land and the pier where the *Restoration* lay without much trouble, provided no one saw her. Margit stood still for a moment and prayed that this wouldn't happen. Then, as she continued walking, she planned her actual boarding of the boat. If the gangplank were down, it would help. Otherwise, she'd have to do some climbing. There were two steps from the railing onto the deck. She would need her wits about her! If she became con-fused, she might stumble toward the gangway leading to the cabin below. She'd better keep her directions straight and move toward the bow. Once she reached the compass and steering wheel she would be safe for the overturned dory was close by. It would probably mean a tight squeeze crawl-ing under it, but she'd manage. Once there, there would be little likelihood that she would be discovered for some time, so narrow was the crack between the edge of the dory and the deck itself.

She became suddenly aware that her heart was beating with

thunderous rapidity and that she was trembling from head to foot. It was eerie down here at the water front. The sound of the wind and the waves frightened her. Every step she took made an alarming clatter against the cobblestones. She thought she heard someone behind her and looked back to see if she were being followed. She started in terror at dark shadows and objects in the distance whose outlines she was unable to make out clearly. But she moved on. Her entire future depended upon keeping up her courage and boarding the *Restoration*.

At last, just ahead of her, she saw the pile of lumber standing out light against the dark background. She had reached the pier where the *Restoration* was moored. For a moment, tears of relief filled her eyes. Then she stiffened. No time to relax. The most crucial test of all confronted her now.

Slowly and with great caution she slipped into the dark shed. She groped along, and was just congratulating herself that she had reached the other end, when suddenly she found herself sprawling at full length on the rough floor. She picked herself up and stood still, straining her ears to catch any sound. All she heard was the continuous roar from the sea and the blowing of the wind. She breathed more freely. Evidently she had the shed to herself.

Again she started to move, even more cautiously, although her eyes had now become accustomed to the complete darkness. She could afford no more stumbling, either here in the shed or after she had boarded the *Restoration*.

After what seemed an inordinately long time for the short distance she had to cover, Margit reached the open pier. She was quite sure it was the *Restoration* that lay to one side of it, in the same position it had been that afternoon. But in order that there be no mistake, she stopped before she tried to board it. And, even though there were no lights aboard, she was able to make out the name of Cornelius Nelson on a chest on deck, close to where the step led down from the rail. Ingrid's brother must have brought the Nelsons to Stavanger so late that their chest had not been put down into the hold.

But now she would have to hurry aboard the vessel. It was the very last, but also the most dangerous part of the entire undertaking. It was unthinkable that the *Restoration* would have been left unguarded for the night. In some way, she would have to elude the person on duty.

There was no gangplank, but it should not be too difficult to get over the narrow gap between the boat and the pier. Her heart was in her mouth as she moved over to the very edge of the pier and took a firm hold of a heavy rope hanging loose along the side of the boat. She pulled herself toward the boat, but just as she felt one foot leaving the pier, she slipped. Both feet touched the water and, for a moment, all seemed lost. Then she realized that she was still grasping the rope, even though she had no footing and was swinging alongside the boat. By carefully lowering herself on the rope, she was able to get back on the pier once more. She would have to start her climb all over again. This time she took her hold much higher on the rope, gave herself a mighty push, turned a somersault, and found herself in a sitting position on the edge of the boat's rail. Holding her breath and trying to avoid making the slightest noise, she eased herself gradually down to the deck. As she crouched against the rail, she realized for the first time that her head was throbbing and there were sharp pains in the lower part of her back. She must have hurt herself either when she stumbled in the shed or while dangling alongside the boat. Well, this was no time for coddling herself. Now for the final effort and, if luck were with her, her goal would be reached.

She started crawling on her hands and knees. As the palms of her hands touched the deck, they burned as if on fire. Of course she had bruised them pulling herself up the rope. No matter, she would have to keep crawling. Her wet shoes bothered her. She slipped them off and managed to jam them into the deep pocket of her skirt. In stocking feet she would be less apt to make a noise.

She was making progress, even though it was slow. She had passed the dangerous place near the gangway leading down into the cabin. She moved on. She could feel the base of the steering wheel. The compass, too, was behind her. The dory must be only inches away. A little more good fortune and she would be under it and safe.

There were sounds from below. Margit stopped, scarcely daring to breathe. She listened so intensely her ears seemed to pull outward. She could hear nothing more. By inches she dragged herself forward on her stomach. She bumped into something hard. At last—it was the dory.

Margit turned over on her back and slid under it. When she was sure she was entirely hidden, she drew a long, deep breath. Then, so completely exhausted that she was able neither to think nor to feel anything more, she closed her eyes and fell fast asleep.

CHAPTER SIX

When Margit opened her eyes, her first sensation was that the ceiling had become amazingly low. Her uncomfortably hard bed at Mistress Catherine's had become much harder. Still more remarkable, it seemed to be swaying or rocking. Margit tried to sit up. Her head bumped against the low ceiling and she fell back, shaken by the pain.

She was wide awake at last. And then she knew. She was aboard the *Restoration*, and the peculiar motion was the rolling of the boat at sea.

There were voices which rose above the roar of the waves. The shrill cry of a child came from a distance.

Still Margit continued to lie under the dory. Something was wrong with her. Every bone in her body ached as though she had received a severe beating. The bump on her head which she had just suffered couldn't have caused all this. Then the reason for the pain dawned on her. She had been lying in a cramped position in the tight space under the dory. On further reflection, she realized that she must have been there for hours. More pain and of a different nature, twisted her stomach. It reminded her that she had not touched food since—yes, it must have been yesterday afternoon. In all her life, her appetite had never failed her, even when she had rebelled against Mistress Catherine's extremely monotonous fare. From the bright light that penetrated into the tiny space where she was lying, it was evident that it must be about noon again now.

Yet the prospect of facing the passengers and the crew on the *Restoration* was an appalling one. What did people do with stowaways at sea? Martha Larson had trimmed down, almost to the ounce, the supplies she was permitting herself to take along and her baggage had been gauged to the square inch. All the others on board must have done the same. Under such circumstances, they could be expected to begrudge every mouthful needed to keep Margit alive during the crossing of the Atlantic Ocean.

Perhaps it would be best to lie where she was and slip into eternity. Mistress Catherine was always preparing herself and her household for death. To her, this life was of little importance in comparison with Paradise.

But Margit was not ready for Mistress Catherine's kind of Paradise. And, in fact, Mistress Catherine herself had on a few occasions expressed grave doubts of Margit's ever getting there.

Besides, if she let herself die, what would become of this dream she had of going to America? And of her determination to deliver Master Cleng's travel notebook to him in person? At the thought of both these calamities, Margit shook herself out of her inertia. She was going to do all she could to go on living.

Now that she was actually on her way to America, it would be a pity not to get at least a glimpse of the Wonder City of New York. No, she wouldn't die yet.

Margit began to move her body a few inches, back and forth, then sideways under the dory. Her muscles became more relaxed, and there was less pain. Gradually, turning her back toward the opening between the dory and the deck, she succeeded in freeing half her body. With more pulling and tugging, her arms were outside her hiding place, too. Finally, she was lying flat, face downward, on the open deck. She put both palms on the deck and, using them to brace herself, she got to her feet. At last, she stood upright. The glare from the ocean and the open sky blinded her, and she stood still, completely bewildered.

In seconds she was surrounded. Men, women and children crowded so close to her that they almost knocked her down. They raised their voices against her in one discordant chorus.

For a moment, Margit had a panicky vision of being trampled under foot and thrown into the sea. Already she was forced to her knees by the pressure of the throng.

"Stand back."

Lars Larson stretched out both arms and the crowd gave way. Then he was at Margit's side.

"Let me help you up," he said kindly, taking hold of both her arms. On her feet once more, she swayed from side to side. Lars Larson led her to an overturned box and set her down on it.

"Martha," he said in a low voice, "I think the child is weak from hunger. Get her some hot tea and flat bread." Then he turned to Cornelius Nelson, whom Margit recognized in the crowd. "There is still fire left in the grate since the last cooking. Help my wife to heat water over it."

Some time later, when Margit sat sipping tea and eating flat bread and cheese, she heard grumbling among the passengers from the other side of the deck.

"What right did she have to steal aboard?"

"We're overcrowded as it is."

"There's not an inch to spare in the cabin."

"Where will she sleep? I can't get along with any less bedding than we are using."

"I'd hate to see her starve, but, after all, she has brought all this trouble upon herself."

Martha Larson, who had been standing close to Margit, moved toward the group at the opposite end of the deck. Margit saw Lars Larson come up to her, and the two spoke together in low tones. Would they advise the captain of the vessel to turn around and sail back to Norway? Margit had no way of knowing how far out to sea the *Restoration* had already sailed. Open water lay all around her.

Martha left Lars Larson's side and went over to the group who were still talking excitedly. "How can you act and speak in such a way?" she asked in clear tones loud enough for Margit to hear every word. "This child is seeking a haven in America, just as every man, woman and child on this boat hopes to. Only she has neither father nor mother to make the journey possible for her, as your own children have."

There was more grumbling. "We aren't responsible for any but our own children."

"None of you has been asked to share anything with Margit," Martha Larson said, raising her voice a little. "My husband and I will share with her as long as our supplies last. If and when they are gone, it will be time enough for the rest of you to worry."

There was dead silence in the group on deck now.

Lars Larson returned to Margit's side. "It was wrong of you to steal aboard," he said, speaking very low. But his tone was mild and there was a suggestion of a smile on his lips.

Martha Larson came over, too. "Margit is a good child," she said. "You know that, Lars. Think how much she helped us those last weeks in Stavanger. And I'll show her how we plan to do things here on board, so she can be of service to us and perhaps to others, too." She took Margit's hand. "But first, child, we must do something about that large bump you have on your head. You must have knocked it against something with considerable force. Sarah and I will put cold compresses on it, and I think the swelling will go down."

Still holding Margit's hand, Martha took her down into the cabin. Almost the entire floor space was taken up with food chests and rolls of bedding. There was the cradle and the hammocks, all strung up close to the ceiling. It was with difficulty that Martha piloted Margit over to their berth. Lars Larson came down almost immediately with a basin of ocean water. The compress which Martha put on Margit's head was cool and it soothed the pain.

"There, that's better," Martha said. "The bump is smaller and will, I hope, disappear entirely before long."

Margit tried to thank her. "Never mind about that," Martha said. "Perhaps now you would like me to tell you a little about how we are managing. As you see, Lars has made this board to fit the length of our bunk. When it is not in use, we can fold up its legs and place it against the wall. It serves as a table, and we use the edge of our bunk as chairs. You and Sarah will sit on two of our covered food containers, which we will take out of the big chest each time we eat. In this way, we shall not be usurping any space down here that ought to be used by someone else. At night, we'll use some of the covers we brought aboard to make up a double bed on the floor beside our bunk. You and Sarah will share it. With the two of you in one bed, it will be easier for you to keep warm, should the nights grow cold before we reach America."

Margit was on the verge of tears. She had not expected such kindness.

"We may have to depend upon some of the others, if our

supplies run out," Martha continued. "But we'll not worry about that until the occasion arises. In the meantime, the families will take turns cooking over the open fire out on deck. Since I often become nauseated in the morning these days, Lars has suggested that he build the fire in the grate and also be the first one using the fire to cook our breakfast. We'll have our porridge and our hot coffee then, since each family will be limited to one hot meal a day. Lars also wants to be on hand right after we have had our breakfast to supervise the rationing of fresh water for the day. Each family is allowed a ration for each of its members. Our share will now be increased, so that you, too, will receive what you need."

"Thank you," was all Margit was able to say.

"We'll have to expect storms," Martha Larson continued. "Then only the men will be allowed on deck. That will mean that the rest of us will be more crowded than ever down here. At such times, great patience and consideration for others will be demanded of us."

"I'll do my best," Margit said.

"Of course you will. And, since you helped with the packing of our food chest, perhaps you won't mind fetching whatever is needed out of it. That will mean a great deal to me."

"I'll be very careful about everything," Margit said eagerly.

Martha smiled. "Of that I have no doubt whatever."

"What time is it now?" Margit asked suddenly.

"Four o'clock in the afternoon. You must have come aboard during the night. The mate, Erickson, says he went below shortly after midnight, so it was probably then."

When it was time for the evening meal, Margit offered to prepare it. Lars Larson took her with him into the hold of the boat to show her where the casks of fresh water and clabbered milk had been stored. Then he carried one of the casks of milk into the cabin and Martha measured out what she considered each person in her group was entitled to have at a meal. From then on, Margit would take over this duty, too. This matter settled, she went into the hold for the first leg of dried goat meat and flat bread, which would make up the rest of the meal. Lars Larson cut paper-thin slices of the meat, according to Martha's directions. She also portioned out the flat bread. She asked Margit to return to the food chest what remained of both the flat bread and the meat.

"It will be best to ration the food right from the start," Martha Larson said. "If we find we are going to have plenty, we can be more generous toward the end of the voyage."

For once, Margit was not hungry. Her head ached, and she was still completely exhausted. Therefore, when the summer night became dark enough to ensure a degree of privacy in the cabin, she was glad to go to bed, settling down with the others.

In Mistress Catherine's home it had been regarded as indecent for a girl to step into a bedroom where there was a man. Margit's training had been strict and the first night aboard she was embarrassed when she removed her dress and hung it over the cradle up near the ceiling. Feeling almost naked in her knitted wool petticoat and underwear, she spread out the sheepskin on the floor. But forty-five others—men, women and children—were preparing for bed in much the same way in the crowded quarters, and Margit was thankful that there was any space at all for her. She was thankful, too, that the limited supply of kerosene aboard the *Restoration* had to be reserved for emergencies, so everyone undressed in the dark.

In spite of her aching body and bruised head, Margit slept soundly all night. When she woke up, she was surprised to see Lars Larson standing close by, holding the steaming coffee kettle in one hand and the kettle of hot porridge in the other. Martha and Sarah were also up and dressed. Margit got her own dress down from the cradle and, her cheeks burning with confusion, put it on with all possible speed.

After the four of them were seated at the folding table, Martha said, "It seems like home, having Margit eating with us, doesn't it, Lars?"

"It certainly does," Lars Larson said enthusiastically.

Margit felt more than grateful. The careful rationing of food made her realize what a sacrifice her presence was going to mean to all three of them.

Fortunately the weather was clear, and the sea was almost calm, with just enough of a breeze to fill the sails. Margit was glad to escape from the cabin where the atmosphere was thick with the odor of food from the many breakfasts, and from the confusion of rolling up bedding on which forty-five passengers had slept during the night, spreading out more for those already suffering from seasickness. She went out on deck and found a place, well away from the others.

Margit settled down to some realistic thinking. Many of the passengers must still feel resentful toward her, even though Lars Larson had put a stop to their grumbling aloud. Lars Larson had pointed out to her, frankly though quietly, she had been at fault in giving way to the impulse that prompted her to steal aboard. It would, therefore, be best to keep her distance from all the passengers, so that those who felt most keenly their righteous wrath might have time to recover a little. Anyway, she was dead tired and it was a relief to lie outstretched on the deck and to feel the healing sunshine warm her aching body.

After a few days, Margit began to feel at home on the *Restoration*. She also began to take a real interest in the people around her. She noticed how bored and unhappy the children were becoming because of the confined and monotonous life on the small vessel. Martha Larson was having increasing difficulty keeping them amused and reasonably quiet.

Late one afternoon, toward the end of an unusually trying day, an entire group of tired and unhappy children crowded at one end of the deck and let out a terrific wail, all at the same time.

Margit went over to them and sat down on the deck. She took a little girl of about five, who was crying more bitterly than the rest, onto her lap.

Using the sleeve of her own dress to wipe the tears of the unhappy child, she asked, "Did you ever hear the story of why all the bridges in Norway can talk?"

The little girl caught her breath, let out two sharp, dry sobs and looked wonderingly up into Margit's face. Margit took advantage of the momentary pause and said quickly, "You see it isn't really the bridges that talk, but the trolls who live under them."

By this time, the other children had grown more quiet, too, and had crowded around Margit. "You see," she continued, "there was once a man who was cruel to his horse and he beat the poor beast most dreadfully. One night when he was crossing the bridge over a stream near his home, the troll living underneath sprayed water on the bridge, making it very slippery. The horse stumbled, sending the bad man into the stream."

Now every child was listening wide-eyed to the story and there was not the slightest sound from any of them.

"The horse returned to the farm where it belonged, but without its owner and the man was never heard of after that."

"But I thought you were going to tell us why the bridges

in Norway can talk," a little boy reminded Margit, a look of real disappointment on his face.

"I'm coming to that," Margit said, anxious to keep the interest she had aroused in her listeners. "When the rest of the trolls heard what their fellow troll had done, they were very angry.

" 'You should have warned the man,' they said. 'If another horse-beater happens to cross your bridge or one of ours, what then?'

"The trolls decided to meet together at the top of Dovre Mountain, which, as you all know, is the highest peak in Norway, and discuss what should be done with cruel horse-beaters. After much debate, it was decided that there should be a warning to all owners of horses in Norway to treat their beasts kindly. Every time a rider crossed a bridge, the troll living underneath it was to call out, '*Stel pent med hesten.*' (Treat the horse kindly.) And so that's just what they do. When a rider starts across a bridge in Norway, the troll begins to call out, '*Stel pent med hesten,*' and continues to warn him until he has reached the other side of the stream."

All the children took a deep breath.

"Of course," Margit went on, "since the trolls have had to breathe in so much damp air, their voices are rather queer, but every rider can understand them. And because of these warnings coming up from underneath the bridges in Norway, horses there are treated more kindly than in any other part of the world."

This time Margit was greeted with cries of "Tell us more. Tell us more." And she did, as happy to be telling the stories as the children were to listen to them.

It was strange how the Bible stories, which Mistress Catherine had forced Margit to read and which, at that time, had seemed uninteresting and unreal, now suddenly came to life.

As if she had actually been present in old Biblical times Margit described Noah and his ark. The children asked endless questions, since they were on the sea themselves, and could picture how crowded Noah's ark must have been with all the animals on board.

Finally Margit got to the story of Leif Ericsson which Master Cleng had told her on his return from America. And now that both she and the children were actually bound for the great fairyland, it seemed of greater significance than when he had told it to her.

Margit started out by saying that all the kings of Norway had been driven out of their kingdoms by the greatest of all kings, Harold Hairfair, who made all Norway into one kingdom. All the kings who were forced to leave settled on the island of Iceland, so that to this day, all people there are the descendants of early kings. One of the bravest of these was a man named Leif Ericsson. He was as much at home on the sea as most people are in their gardens. And on one of his voyages, he landed on a faraway shore, which turned out to be a part of what is known now as the great United States.

"So you see, children," Margit concluded, "you are all bound for the country which was actually discovered by one of our very own Norwegians."

Margit looked up. Men and women surrounded the children, who were sitting hunched over on the deck. Expressions of gratitude, approval, interest and—yes—admiration showed on their faces.

"You are a very good storyteller," Lars Larson said. "I never appreciated what a great person Leif Ericsson must have been until I heard what you had to say about him."

Lars Larson's words were music in Margit's ears. They expressed what she had seen in the faces of the grownups as they stood listening to her, and what the children had already demonstrated to her in innumerable ways: that they considered her one of them. And best of all, she felt that now at last she was forgiven by the passengers and crew of the *Restoration* for having stolen aboard their vessel. She was thankful and very, very happy.

CHAPTER SEVEN

Margit sat crouched on the floor, each arm clutched around a terrified child pressed against her side. In the dim light of the cabin, she could feel rather than see the bodies of mothers, hunched over their little ones to protect them against any loose objects that might crash down upon them because of the pitching and tossing of the ship. Margit herself was frozen with fear.

For days a terrifying storm had been raging on the Atlantic. With increasing violence, the wind and waves and torrential rains had given vent to their fury upon the helpless little vessel. Now the storm had reached almost hurricane proportions and the timbers of the *Restoration* creaked and groaned. It seemed as if at any minute it would crumble like an eggshell and be thrown to the mercies of the angry sea.

During what seemed to be last moments on earth, Margit remembered Mistress Catherine's warnings against leaving the place where God had placed one. Could it be that God was visiting punishment upon the hapless passengers and crew of the *Restoration* because they had been guilty of this sin? And were the wages of this sin to be an end for all of them in a watery grave? Margit shuddered to think of what might be awaiting her in the hereafter, for not only had she sinned with all the others, but she had transgressed even more by stealing aboard.

Someone was coming down from the deck. Lars Larson groped his way across the cabin and stood beside his wife's bunk.

It seemed as if he were listening for something. Or was he waiting to tell some terrible news? Perhaps the crew, in their frantic efforts to keep their boat afloat, had all been washed overboard. Margit shuddered. If this had happened, the last ray of hope was lost, for the boat left floundering aimlessly would quickly be overturned and submerged by the onrush of surging water.

Then speaking low, but in a firm voice that could be heard above the roar of the waves, Lars Larson said, "Let us pray."

Margit heard deep breathing all around her. A child whimpered and was hushed by its mother.

"Dear God, our Father," Lars Larson said, "it would appear that these Thy children are in sore straits this day. But we know now, as always, that Thou art watching over us with loving care. If Thou hast work for us in the strange land whither we had hoped to be free the more to carry out Thy will, then we ask Thee to guide us so that we may reach our destination. We place our trust in Thee and know that in Thy love and tender mercy we have nothing to fear, should Thou have other plans for us."

Something—it must have been a miracle—had happened to everyone in the cabin. The mothers sat upright. The children relaxed. Margit loosened her hold on the two children she had been guarding. The tension had eased.

Then suddenly Margit cried out, "God, please save Martha and her baby. It hasn't even lived yet." She had blurted out her cry without a second's forethought. It had come from her heart. For the first time in her life, Margit had really prayed, prayed with faith that a loving Father would hear, would answer her prayer.

"Our Father Which art in Heaven," Lars Larson began softly, "Hallowed be Thy Name, Thy kingdom come, Thy will be done on earth as it is in Heaven." From every corner of the cabin came the sweet chorus, repeating the prayer. Margit found herself framing the words with her lips.

When the prayer ended, Lars Larson left as quietly as he had come. The storm continued, but the timbers had ceased their groaning and moaning. Little by little, the wind died down. The waves lost their power. The rain stopped. Children slept. Women wept in silent gratitude.

Margit sat in stunned awe. She had heard and read in her Bible about Christ's calming the sea. Always to her it had seemed an interesting but unbelievable fairy tale. Now there was not any doubt in her mind as to the truth of the story. It had happened as it was told in the Bible. And she, herself, had just witnessed a repetition of this miracle.

A while later, Erickson, the mate, came down into the cabin and said that the deck had been wiped off and was fairly dry.

Most of the children, exhausted by the ordeal through which they had so recently passed, continued to sleep, and the mothers, glad of the respite, remained quiet with them. Margit and a few others climbed the ladder and came out into the fresh air. Feeling the urge to be alone, she went to the far end of the deck and sat down by herself. The sea was still gray but the waves were low and rolling and harmless, and the sky above was shaking off its heavy clouds. Small openings of bright blue began to appear. By nightfall, there was a clear sunset and many of the passengers, like Margit, stretched out on deck for a good relaxing sleep.

It must have been well toward morning, although it was still dark, when Margit woke up. She became aware of a commotion, and she got up and went down into the cabin to see what was happening.

Lars Larson, with the help of Cornelius Nelson, was unfastening the cradle from its place up against the ceiling. Then he hung up a sheepskin robe, which completely shut off the bunk in which Martha was lying. Carrie Nelson and Sarah went behind the improvised curtain. Some of the mothers gathered up their children and went on deck. Others were either too ill from seasickness or too exhausted from the ordeal of the storm or were kept in the cabin by sick children. No one spoke. For a few seconds, Margit stood, uncertain what to do. Then slowly and on tiptoe, she walked to the ladder, climbed back on deck and again sought out the spot almost under the dory where she could be alone.

Again God was answering her prayer. Martha's baby was being born. Up to now, birth and death had been foreign experiences to Margit. To be sure, lambs and kittens and puppies and calves and other offspring of the animals on the place arrived at frequent intervals. Margit had cried bitterly when *Glad Gut*, her pet dog, had been killed by a runaway team of horses. But the human beings in Mistress Catherine's household lived on and on as if they had always been there and would continue to be there as far into the future as she could imagine.

On a few occasions, neighbors came for Mistress Catherine and there were whispered exchanges between her and Gunda. Then Mistress Catherine left in great haste and was gone for several days. On her return from these mysterious visits, there was more whispering. Soon after that, Margit would hear that a new baby had arrived at the home which

Mistress Catherine had visited. But for some reason, which was never clear to Margit, the news of the actual birth of a baby was something which Mistress Catherine felt should be kept a dark secret, a subject which it was not proper to discuss.

Now that Martha Larson's baby was expected at any moment, Margit controlled her emotions with great difficulty. She was so happy at the thought of having a real, live baby aboard and perhaps in her own arms that she could not sleep.

The sea was almost calm now, and the deep blue sky was dotted with myriads of stars. As Margit lay staring up at them, they seemed to grow brighter and brighter. She thought of something Ingrid's mother had once told her: that the souls of people who died ascended into heaven and that ever afterward they kept watch from the stars over their loved ones whom they had left behind on earth. An orphan didn't have any loved ones. Yet every child must have had parents to start with and, however short a time they might have been permitted to live together, the parents must have loved their child.

As Margit continued to gaze up into the sky, she tried to imagine from which star her father and mother might be watching over her. She chose an especially bright one for her mother's soul. As it twinkled against the deep blue background, Margit had a feeling that her mother's soul was calling to her. She felt something hot and wet on her cheek, and she brushed it off with the sleeve of her dress.

"Mother, were people waiting for me just as we are waiting for the Larson's baby tonight?" she whispered.

People were stirring around her. She heard Lars Larson's voice. "We have a beautiful daughter," he announced, a joyful ring in his voice. "Martha and I have already decided to

name her Margaret Allen, in honor of the wonderful mother
of our great English Quaker missionary, William Allen."

Margaret Allen Larson. What a fortunate little girl she
was! Two loving parents like Lars and Martha Larson, and
a loving aunt like Sarah Larson. It wouldn't matter that Sarah
was deaf and dumb with all the love she had to shower on
the little girl. She would be blessed, too, with all the love
of the passengers on the *Restoration*, in whose midst she
would grow up when the colony was established in America.
No child living could ask for a more wonderful future.

It was well into the forenoon of the following day when
Lars Larson invited Margit to come down into the cabin
and see his little daughter. Since the sky had again become
very overcast, it was by the light of the tiny kerosene lamp
that Margit for the first time in her life stood looking down
at a newborn baby. Little Margaret Allen had been bathed
and dressed in swaddling clothes and laid in the cradle beside her mother's bunk. Suddenly Margit was so moved by
a feeling of awe and reverence that, without thinking, she
fell to her knees beside the cradle. The sleeping child in the
cradle reminded her for all the world of the pictures she had
seen of the Christ Child lying in the manger in Bethlehem.

"How do you like our little daughter?" Martha Larson
asked softly from her bunk.

"She's—she's beautiful," Margit gasped.

For days after Margaret Allen's arrival, Margit could think
of nothing else. The first thing in the morning when Lars
Larson brought the hot coffee and porridge for his little
group, Margit took it upon herself to move the cradle well
out of the way. Each one sat with his bowl of porridge bal-
anced on his lap and his coffee cup on the floor. For with
the cradle moved down from its perch near the ceiling, there

was not space enough even for the collapsible table Lars Larson had made. After the meal was over, Margit sat on the floor beside the cradle and rocked the baby.

"You are spoiling her shamefully," Martha said. But she smiled as she spoke and Margit knew that her words were not meant as a reprimand.

Margit slept so lightly after Margaret Allen's birth that she wakened at her slightest movement. Often she rocked the cradle before anyone else knew that the baby had stirred.

"You are a great help, caring for little Margaret Allen," Martha Larson told Margit after a week had passed. "Sarah and I have so much knitting to do that we appreciate having you with the baby."

Margit glowed with pleasure. It was wonderful to be praised for something you would rather do than anything else in the world. When Margaret Allen was asleep in her cradle, Margit would sit on the edge of Martha's bunk and look at the baby for hours.

When she was awake, Margit either rocked her or sat on the floor holding her. In all her life, Margit had never owned a doll. Now she had a real live one with her day and night.

The weather again suddenly turned stormy and almost everyone on board became very seasick, including Martha and Sarah Larson. In spite of her illness, Martha kept the baby in the bunk with her because of the pitching of the boat, for she could not risk having her tossed out of the cradle. Only the men were allowed on deck to help the crew.

Margit missed caring for the baby so much that she was utterly miserable. In fact, except for her first day aboard the *Restoration*, this was the most unhappy time of the entire voyage. In the crowded cabin, there could be almost no moving about. Margit kept to her sheep pelt on the floor. When the pitching of the vessel became so violent that she was afraid she might be struck by some loose object, she crouched by the Larsons' bunk and clung to it with all her strength. It was well into September now, and the nights had become long and cold. Margit, like all the other passengers, slept in all her outer clothing in an effort to keep warm.

Finally this storm, too, seemed to have spent itself, and comparative calm settled over the ocean. The passengers were able to get up from their beds and the monotony of life aboard the vessel was resumed.

For Margit, however, life was no longer monotonous. She was witnessing the development of a newborn baby so lovely that only the angels in heaven could be compared with her. Mistress Catherine had only tolerated the presence of little children in her home when it could not be avoided. As for coddling any young thing on her place—including friendly puppies, wobbly calves and the offspring of the other animals —she considered such foolishness a waste of time, and she discouraged it as much as she could.

Martha Larson spent hours holding her baby and caring for her tenderly and lovingly. Every time Sarah Larson touched the baby, it was done gently and caressingly. As for Lars Larson, the mere mention of his tiny daughter brought a light of pride and joy into his eyes. Margit basked in the warmth of so much affection and she, too, adored the baby. Nothing made her happier than to be permitted to hold Margaret Allen while Martha and Sarah were knitting or performing other tasks.

As time passed and no mention was made of having Margaret Allen baptized, Margit grew troubled. To Mistress Catherine, infant baptism was as important as life itself. In fact, even more important, for it also ensured the expectation of a life in the hereafter. The godparents took the vow of faith in the Trinity and promised to see that the child be brought up in this faith, should the real parents die before he grew to maturity. Until the godparents had taken these vows for the infant, and water had been sprinkled on its head, and the blessing had been given, all people were heathens to Mistress Catherine's way of thinking. There was no hope for the salvation of their souls. So strong was her belief on this subject that, in emergencies when no minister of the Gospel was available, she had been known to baptize newborn infants herself in order to save them from eternal damnation.

The storm had impressed on Margit the possibility of the baby's sudden death. However fine people the Larsons were, they must be mistaken if they failed to consider this sacrament necessary for their child. In any case, it seemed to Margit too vital a matter to take any chances by omitting it.

So she decided that she, herself, when the opportunity presented itself, must perform the ritual. She might not be as efficient about it as Mistress Catherine had been. But she had witnessed so many baptisms in the Tysvaer parish church that she knew exactly how the ceremony should be performed and she could repeat everything that had to be said, word for word.

One evening Lars Larson said that, if the weather was favorable the following morning, Margit might take the baby up on deck for a little while. At once it occurred to Margit that this would offer the opportunity she had been waiting for to baptize little Margaret Allen. She wouldn't dare risk getting water out of the ocean. Besides, who ever heard of baptizing a baby with salt water? She would save her allotment of fresh water and somehow get it up on deck with her while the baby was being carried there. Then, after they were settled and no one was about, she would baptize little Margaret Allen.

The morning dawned bright and still. Everything seemed favorable. Lars Larson carried the cradle up on deck, and Martha brought the baby. She tucked her tenderly under the down quilt and turned the cradle so that the sun would not shine directly into the baby's eyes. "It will do her a world of good to breathe some of this fresh sea air and get some sunshine, too," Martha said. "And I know that she will be absolutely safe in your care, Margit."

Margit felt guilty for not telling her of the baptism. But since it was for Margaret Allen's good, she would have to risk deceiving her this once.

Lars Larson had placed the cradle close to the dory where it was protected from any chance gusts of wind. Most of the passengers had chosen the opposite end of the deck, where they could enjoy the fresh breeze. Margit had succeeded in holding her cup of fresh water under the skirt of her dress, and had hidden it under the dory. Everything had turned out better than Margit had hoped.

Now the moment for the actual baptism had arrived. It should be very simple. She would do it at once.

Margit repeated word for word the baptism ritual, just as she had heard it from the lips of the parish minister. She asked the questions about renouncing the devil and believing in the Holy Trinity and about living according to this faith. To each question, she gave the affirmative answer expected of the godmother. Then she went over to the dory for her cup of precious fresh water. She carried it over to the cradle and placed it carefully on the baby's pillow. Then, repeating the words, "Margaret Allen, I baptize thee in the name of

—" she raised the baby's head with one hand and was about to dip her other one into the cup and sprinkle the water over Margaret Allen's head, when the cup tipped and spilled the water over her face instead. The baby screamed. Margit picked her up and tried to soothe her as she brushed the little face against the front of her dress. People came rushing from the far end of the deck. Lars and Martha Larson were both there in an instant, and Martha took the baby from Margit's arms.

"I didn't mean to hurt her," was all Margit could say.

"Of course, you didn't," Martha said kindly. She glanced at the overturned cup on Margaret Allen's pillow. "Don't feel badly. She was only a little frightened. A few drops of water won't hurt her. It's time for her to be brought downstairs now anyway."

Lars Larson carried the cradle back down into the cabin. The other passengers returned to their post on the breezy end of the deck. Margit remained behind the dory.

Martha's kind words had eased her feeling of shame and sorrow at having frightened the baby, but she knew that she had failed miserably in fulfilling her mission. For a moment, she was filled with deep regret. Then the picture of Lars Larson and Martha, as they stood beside the cradle only a few minutes ago, all tender concern for their baby, came back to her. If ever anyone loved anyone else, Lars and Martha loved their child.

It would take wiser and older heads than hers, Margit decided, to pass judgment on what people did and believed. She only knew that the Larsons were good and kind. From the first day she had met them, they had brought warmth and happiness into her life. They were sharing everything they had with her now. And they were making it possible for all the passengers on the *Restoration* to migrate to America, where they would enjoy opportunities they had never known in Norway, and where they could worship God according to their own beliefs. This must be what was meant by loving one's neighbor, and she hoped God would take all these things into consideration.

CHAPTER EIGHT

One morning when Lars Larson brought hot coffee and porridge for breakfast as usual, he announced, "Well, ladies,
enjoy your leisure while you may. In only a short while now,
back to the kitchen you go."

Martha, who had just laid the baby in the cradle, looked
up at him inquiringly. "Do you mean that you want Margit
or me to take over the cooking on deck?" she asked.

A broad smile spread over her husband's face. "Oh, no,"
he said. "I'm not surrendering that honorable post until I
have to. What I'm trying to tell you is that before long now,
we shall be landing in America."

Margit was too much excited to eat. As soon as she had
helped to clear away the breakfast things, she went up on
deck. Since last night, a complete change had taken place
in the atmosphere up there. Members of the crew were scur-
rying around. Captain Helland was calling out orders. There
was singing at the far end of the deck. And down in the
forecastle, where the crew slept, there was loud talking and
laughter.

Margit let her gaze wander out to sea. Nothing had changed
there. The rolling waves met the horizon all around the *Res-*

toration. Up above, the blue sky was dotted with fleecy white clouds. In the East, the sun was rising, giving promise of a mild, pleasant day.

Margit's thoughts went back to the night she boarded the *Restoration* at the dead of night. Much had happened since, some of it rather difficult, more that was pleasant. Nevertheless, she would be glad when the voyage came to an end.

These reflections brought to mind the original purpose for which she had broken away from her life at Mistress Catherine's. Now she would soon arrive in America to deliver the notebook to Master Cleng. Instinctively her hand dropped into her pocket. Yes, the notebook was still there, sewed securely in the very bottom of the deep pocket. She would be careful that it didn't fall out, for it was most important that she have it ready to hand to Master Cleng the minute she found him.

What would he say when he saw her? How would he react to her coming to America without his permission? He would be surprised, of that there could be no doubt. As for the rest—well, she would have to hope that he would be pleased to receive the travel notebook and that he would not be too angry with her for stealing aboard the *Restoration* and arriving in America as a stowaway.

Deep inside, she was glad for what she had done. It was going to be the most thrilling experience of her life to set foot on the wonderful land about which she had heard so many amazing tales.

Finally the moment arrived. Word spread over the *Restoration* that land had been sighted. Everyone rushed out on deck. Margit trailed behind the others, not because she was not just as excited as they were to get her first glimpse of

America, but because she felt that everyone on board had a better right than she did to this thrilling sight.

The last child had had his turn at the field glasses when Erickson, the first mate, handed them to Margit. Her hand shook as she held them up to her eyes. There it was—only a dark line, scarcely thicker than the width of a pencil. But it was the all-important line that separated the seemingly endless expanse of ocean and the domed sky. Soon this pencil-like line would expand and become the huge wonderful America.

"We're almost in America! We're almost in America!" could be heard from stem to stern of the ship. There was no cooking that morning. The last sticks of wood were used to keep the fire burning in order to take the chill off the ocean water for over fifty baths. So intent was everyone on making himself presentable for the landing that the omission of food and the lack of privacy for the baths seemed of no consequence whatever.

Margit took her well-filled drinking cup of lukewarm tea water and made her way to the dory. As far back as she could remember, she had never been completely undressed in the presence of anyone else. And now by a series of maneuvers under the dory and frugally making use of the water in her cup, she managed her bath with at least a degree of privacy.

When she emerged from her hiding place, she came upon Carrie Nelson who was leaning over the edge of the boat, dipping water out of the ocean. "I've used up all the warm water for the children's baths," she told Margit. "Now I'm going to try to rub the worst soiled spots off their clothes. But it's really hopeless. What wouldn't I give to have a fresh outfit to put on each of them before we land. At least for the girls. People don't expect boys to look so clean."

To Margit, these last weeks without bathing had been nothing short of calamitous. Even after her attempted bath, she felt little better. According to Mistress Catherine's teachings, an unwashed body housed a black soul. It was a good thing Mistress Catherine couldn't see her now. But Master Cleng would be seeing her very soon, and she dreaded to think of what a bad impression her unattractive appearance would make. For he did notice appearances. He wouldn't have thought of giving her the blue velvet ribbon to wear in her hair like the girls in America, if he hadn't paid attention to how they looked. Well, she had done the best she could, so she wouldn't let herself worry any more about that problem.

The wind seemed bent on prolonging the suspense, for it refused to blow any breath into the sails and the vessel made almost no headway. No one bothered about meals, and people wandered aimlessly about the deck, straining their eyes to see if the pencil-like mark on the horizon wouldn't soon become a substantial shore line.

At last the miracle happened. Shades of varying colors from white to a deep gray, green and brown, red and yellow caught the attention of the watchers. Suddenly there was a great commotion. Captain Helland ascended his bridge. Word went around that he was about to signal those on land that the *Restoration* was ready to dock. It would, therefore, be appreciated if a tugboat could be sent out to tow the vessel safely into the pier. Three shots, fired in quick succession, gave the message.

The passengers on board stared anxiously at the shore line. Soon a tugboat began moving toward them. When it came closer, one of the men pointed in the direction of the *Restoration*.

"They have seen our Norwegian flag," Captain Helland

called out. "Cleng Peerson has, no doubt, asked them to be on the lookout for us."

Margit watched as the small craft came alongside. Lines were cast out and the crew, under Captain Helland's direction, fastened the ropes that held the two boats together. Then, slowly and carefully, the tug started to pull the *Restoration* toward shore.

Long before they had reached the pier, Margit had singled out Master Cleng. It was not difficult, for, as usual, he was wearing his fur cap, his long black cloak and his high boots. The sight of his familiar figure brought a lump to Margit's throat. He was the only person in America who linked her old life in Norway to the new one which was about to begin. Never, in all her life, had she been so glad to see him as she was at this very moment. Her first impulse was to crowd as close as possible to the place where the gangplank would be lowered and as soon as the boat docked, rush forward to greet him. But at once she realized that she would not dare to do that.

For one thing there were people on the boat who, by the nature of their importance, should be among the first to land. Captain Helland might not want to leave his ship, but she would have to step back and give him a chance to do so. Then there was Lars Larson and his family, whom Master Cleng would certainly be most anxious to welcome. After all, Lars Larson was the one who had made the voyage possible. John Stene, who with Lars Larson, had shared the major expense of buying the boat and reconditioning it to make it seaworthy, should also be one of the first to land. Of course, Master Cleng would be concerned, too, about his sister Carrie Nelson and her family.

But after all these had had an opportunity to walk down the gangplank, Margit decided, she had better put in her appearance. She would not give Master Cleng the impression that she was hanging back because she was ashamed of being there. If she did not wait too long before landing, the Larsons would still be close by to put in a good word for her and help her with any difficulty that might arise.

It seemed important to figure out ahead of time her exact words of greeting. She held Master Cleng's notebook firmly in her hand and, as soon as she set foot on the pier, there would be no beating around the bush in delivering it to him. She would hand it to him then and there, just as she had pictured herself doing it hundreds of times during the voyage.

As soon as the gangplank had been lowered, Margit edged toward it, but remained well behind those to land first. Best to keep out of Master Cleng's sight until her turn came.

Lars Larson was the first one to reach the pier. He carried little Margaret Allen in his arms and when Master Cleng came forward to greet him, she heard Lars Larson say, "What do you think of this little passenger we took aboard while we were in the middle of the Atlantic Ocean?"

He pulled the blanket aside and Master Cleng bent down and kissed the tiny face. Then he exclaimed loud enough for those still aboard the *Restoration* to hear, "Welcome to the shores of the Promised Land, young lady. May you enjoy a long and happy life here with your wonderful parents."

How like Master Cleng it was to demonstrate his affection. But Mistress Catherine would have been disgusted with what she would have considered an indication of weakness. She often spoke with disdain of the open expressions of affection which Ingrid's mother showered upon her children.

John Stene followed Martha Larson and after them came the Nelson family. According to her plan, it was now time for Margit to slip into line.

"Couldn't I help you with some of your luggage?" Margit asked Mrs. Rossedahl, who came immediately behind the Nelsons.

"Thank you," Mrs. Rossedahl said, stepping back and setting down a huge bundle of bedding. "We didn't think we had much, but carrying it becomes burdensome."

Margit picked up the bundle.

"You might as well walk between my husband and me," Mrs. Rossedahl said. "Once on the pier, he will get someone to help us move it to the place Cleng Peerson will have for us to stay."

Just as she reached the bottom of the gangplank, Margit, with her free hand, took from her pocket the precious notebook. And the minute she set foot on the pier, she dropped the cumbersome bundle. Mr. Rossedahl shook hands with Master Cleng and then busied himself with the family's luggage.

Margit's great moment had come!

"Master Cleng," she said, doing her best to keep her voice steady. "Here is your travel notebook. I found it just after you had left."

She thrust the notebook into his hand.

For a moment Master Cleng seemed too stunned to speak. Then he said, "How did *you* get here?"

"Mistress Catherine gave me permission to come."

Master Cleng regarded Margit sternly. "The Ninth Commandment is a very important one," he said. "You know better than to think I will believe that."

"Well, she gave me permission to go to Stavanger to help the Larsons get ready for sailing. I thought at first I'd get Lars Larson to deliver the notebook. But when I went down to help him with their luggage aboard the *Restoration* and— and I saw what a beautiful ship it was—and—"

"Go on."

"And I thought how in a short while it would be in America and—"

"So you just stayed aboard."

The stern look on Master Cleng's face had gradually relaxed. Margit gained confidence as she went along. "And the dory—under it—seemed such a good place to—"

Mrs. Rossedahl and her children were pressing from behind. Margit stepped aside and Master Cleng's attention was diverted in greeting the other passengers who were disembarking.

Margit heaved a deep sigh of relief. The crucial moment was over. Here she was on American soil, or at least on the pier where she could reach it by taking a few steps. As for Master Cleng, for the present she would keep out of his way as much as possible and let him recover from the shock of seeing her. After the last passenger had come down the gangplank, Master Cleng led the group toward the end of the pier. Margit brought up the rear with a few stragglers. They entered a long, low building, and a man came up to Master Cleng. Their lively conversation could be heard easily, but Margit could not understand a single word they were saying. Then it dawned on her. She was in America now, and she would be experiencing this difficulty right along, for, of course, English was the language spoken. Why hadn't she thought of this? Then and there Margit decided that she would do everything she could to learn this strange language quickly.

"The man is here to help get you to places where you will stay while you remain in New York," Master Cleng said at last in Norwegian. "You have all been invited to be the guests of friends of mine until we leave for our final destination."

Again Margit lingered with those at the far edge of the

group, but she was careful to keep Master Cleng plainly in sight. As he walked along, followed by the passengers of the *Restoration*, he reminded Margit of a shepherd leading his flock to safety. But with the increasing crowds they were encountering, Margit realized that she might easily become a stranded sheep.

Lars Larson walked beside Cleng and they were talking earnestly but in voices too low to be heard by anyone else. Margit felt certain that Lars Larson was filling in the details of how she had crossed the Atlantic Ocean as a stowaway. If only she had one real friend with whom she could discuss her sudden feeling of embarrassment. Now that she saw how busy Master Cleng was, looking after more than fifty people he had encouraged to migrate and for whose welfare he had made himself personally responsible, he seemed to have become remote, almost a stranger. Suddenly Margit felt herself terribly alone and a little frightened. Then she braced herself. She wouldn't be seeing much of New York City if she started whining like a self-pitying baby!

The group had left the building and were standing on a corner, waiting to cross the street. Margit gazed wide-eyed around her. She had not imagined that, in all the world, there were so many horses and vehicles and people as were passing by at that very moment. Even though the traffic had temporarily halted when Master Cleng started to cross the street, Margit's heart was in her mouth for fear she might be trampled before she arrived safely on the other side.

But once on the sidewalk again, Margit feasted her eyes. Women and young girls, dressed as only queens and princesses in her imagination had ever been, strolled in a large, beautiful garden, or what Margit took to be one. Most of them carried bright-colored umbrellas to match their costumes. Since it was not raining, Margit took it that they must be trying to ward off the unusually warm sun. To her, this seemed absolutely incredible, too, for in Norway the sunshine was thought to be as precious as life itself. It was a beautiful sight, this extravagant display of color. The costumes were all shades of red and pink, yellow and lavender, blue and green, contrasting with the deeper green of the grass and the rich brown and gold and maroon of the leaves on the trees. And over all was the azure dome of the sky in which the sun blazed like a gigantic, brilliant jewel. At this time of year in Norway, the ground would have turned a dull brown and the pine trees a somber green, if everything were not already covered with snow and the sun hidden behind a low curtain of gloomy gray clouds. As for the people themselves, the bitter winds from the mountains and the sea would have already forced them into drab, heavy winter clothing from which they would not emerge until the short nights and long days of spring and summer again drew them out of their cocoons.

So engrossed had Margit been with drinking in the beauty of this strange wonderland that she had forgotten all else. Someone tapped her on the shoulder. She turned to face Master Cleng.

"We missed you," he said. "All the others followed me to the place where our hosts were waiting to take them to their homes. What have you been doing?"

"It's all so beautiful, Master Cleng," Margit breathed softly. "The people and the trees and the flowers and the grass and the sun. You never made me understand what a beautiful place America is."

Master Cleng chuckled. Then his face became grave. "Come. It is not the thing for a young girl like you to stand gaping on the streets of New York."

He took Margit's arm and they started to walk at a brisk pace.

This was a new Master Cleng, strangely different from the man she had known in Norway. He was firm, he was full of energy and he was masterful. People listened to what he said and they followed him. Was this how all people who migrated to America changed? Or was it simply because he was no longer under the domination of Mistress Catherine?

They came to a place where a man stood beside a one-seater buggy. Master Cleng spoke a few words to him in English. The man helped Margit climb into the buggy. Then he got in beside her.

"This man will take you to the house where you are going to stay," Master Cleng said. "Remain there until I come."

There was that masterful manner again! Margit felt fear and loneliness tugging at her heart.

As the horse trotted along, Margit tried to imagine just how Master Cleng felt about her unexpected arrival. He had offered no word of understanding, no word of encouragement, nothing to indicate any plans for her future. He had not even thanked her for delivering the precious notebook personally. If he continued to show this domineering attitude toward her and were to demand that she return to Norway, it would be almost impossible to disobey him.

Then Margit thought of Master Cleng's invariable kindness and gentleness to herself and Ingrid back in Norway. It had seemed to her that once or twice today she had detected his old manner beneath his stern exterior. Surely no one could have changed so completely in such a short time, even though the Atlantic Ocean did separate his old life from this new one. In time he would be as warm and friendly as he had always been.

With this comforting conclusion, Margit was able to think more clearly. She had achieved the seemingly impossible by obtaining Mistress Catherine's permission to get as far as

Stavanger. She had managed by using her own wits to accomplish the almost unthinkable feat of crossing the Atlantic Ocean. Having now arrived in this wonderland, what was to prevent a further miracle that would make her as successful as those other young Norwegian women Master Cleng had told about who came to America to seek their fortunes? At least, it was a hope to cling to, an ambition to work for.

CHAPTER NINE

The morning after Margit's arrival, she awakened with a vague sensation of being in a flower garden filled with sweet-smelling blossoms. Returning to full consciousness, she touched the smooth, white sheet under which she had been sleeping. She brushed her nose against it and found that this was the source of the fragrance. She stretched her body at full length. She had never imagined that her first cause for joy in America would be lying in a clean bed after having been given the scrubbing of her life.

Mrs. Bronson Smith, the tiny, wiry, white-haired lady to whose home Margit had been brought, had received her with smiles and a flow of incomprehensible words. Then she had gone into action. She stripped Margit of every stitch of her filthy clothing, scoured her body and scrubbed her matted hair with frothy soap suds. Finally she had supplied her with cotton underwear, including two voluminous petticoats, and a blue cotton dress, all of which would have fitted her better had they been considerably smaller. Yet it was a relief to be wearing comfortable, clean clothes, better suited to the warm weather in New York. Since Mrs. Bronson Smith was such a very tiny person, Margit thought of the trouble she must have gone to in securing clothes large enough for her guest.

As far as Margit had been able to determine, Mrs. Bronson Smith lived alone in the large, rambling, old house, with only her canary and two large white cats for companionship. Yet all were so sociable and articulate that the huge rooms resounded with their various means of communication.

Margit got out of bed and dressed hurriedly. Lolling in bed wasn't going to show her any of the sights of the most exciting city in the world. Moreover, inviting odors came from downstairs, and from the appetizing food served on her arrival, Margit knew there would be something very good awaiting her now.

In the kitchen, the two white cats were lying on the window sill, basking in the morning sunshine. The canary was cheerfully singing from its cage just above them. Mrs. Smith was flitting about, looking into shining pots and pans, and making innumerable trips into the adjoining dining room. By means of pantomime, Margit and Mrs. Smith did very well, and Margit ate a breakfast such as she had never consumed in all her life. Also by pantomime, Margit understood that Mrs. Smith much preferred to do all her own work including making Margit's bed and washing the dishes. Margit made no serious effort to dissuade her. She might as well go out on the front porch and see what the neighborhood was like.

The houses on the street looked very much like Mrs. Smith's. There were no people around except for some small children playing with a dog. How she would love to take a walk and find out what else was to be seen in this part of the city! Of course, Master Cleng had told her to stay at Mrs. Bronson Smith's until he came, but he couldn't have meant for her to remain housebound. The weather was far too beautiful for that. Ignoring a twinge of uneasiness, Margit started down the street.

After walking only a short distance, she found that the landscape had changed entirely. She saw more and more people and there were more horses and vehicles. She was intrigued by elegant carriages, each driven by a man in uniform on a high seat and with beautifully dressed people sitting in back, facing one another. These people must have hundreds of American dollars to be able to afford such luxuries.

As Margit walked along, she was amazed at the great number and variety of churches she was passing. Some had high spires, some crosses, some nothing at all except a signboard out front with a black background and gilt letters, the only word of which she could read was *Jesus*. Some of the buildings had no distinguishing features. They were long, low buildings with high steps in front and she guessed that they, too, were used for religious worship. A few churches had statues in their gardens and there were people going in and coming out of them, in spite of the fact that it was not Sunday. She saw women in black flowing robes and white-faced bonnets around two or three of these buildings.

All this was strange and exciting. Back in Norway in the parish of Tysvaer, there was only the state Lutheran Church and everyone was supposed to attend it on Sundays, and church holidays such as Good Friday, Easter Monday and Ascension Day. At all other times the parish church was securely locked, children were forbidden to go inside the gate of the fence surrounding it and older people were discouraged from loitering there.

With so many churches in America, Margit mused, how did a person decide which one to attend? Did people visit all of them and then select the one they liked best?

Then the landscape changed again. There were carts loaded with fruits and vegetables, shabby two-wheel buggies with shabbily dressed men sitting in them. Here the buildings were flush with the street, and their fronts were of glass. Things were becoming intensely interesting and Margit slowed her pace.

A crowd had gathered around one of the windows and she joined it, edging her way closer to see what was attracting their attention. It was shoes. Inside the window were arranged pairs and pairs of them. There were large ones and small ones, high boots and slippers. Margit had never seen such an array of shoes in all her life. Some were trimmed with buckles, some with bows. Some were white, some brown, some red, some blue. Until now, Margit had thought that all shoes were made in a harness and shoe shop like the one on Mistress Catherine's estate.

As Margit stood admiring the magnificent display, she singled out a pair of red slippers which looked to be about her size. They were trimmed with shining gilt buckles and bows of shimmering red satin. If only she dared go inside and ask to have them tried on her feet. Just the feel of them once would allow her to wear them for years in her imagination. Margit looked down ruefully at her own clumsy, Norwegian boots. Mrs. Smith had not been able to supply her with American shoes large enough for her feet. Again Margit gazed longingly at the red slippers in the window. Then the crowd jostled her away and they were gone from sight.

Master Cleng was right, Margit thought, when he told his fabulous tales about the immense wealth of Americans. Wherever she looked the luxuries displayed were staggering: tall buildings, windows full of things she could not have conceived in her wildest dreams; people wearing clothes that must have cost a fortune; carriages and other vehicles that must have cost vast sums of money; and horses that farmers back in Norway would have traveled for miles just to see.

Finally Margit's stomach reminded her that a good deal of

time had elapsed since the substantial breakfast Mrs. Smith had served her. She had better retrace her steps in a hurry in order not to miss the noon meal. She had the impression that Mrs. Smith was as rigid in the timing of her work as she was in the manner of doing it.

Margit started back the way she had come. She would loiter no more. The first few shops seemed familiar, but after she had gone a block or two more she knew that the buildings were ones she had not passed before. She must have turned a corner without realizing it. Perhaps if she kept walking she might come to familiar landmarks.

There were shabby red brick buildings with swarms of ragged, dirty children playing on the walks or in the streets. Lines of laundry were strung from one building to another. The smell of cooking blew out of open windows but the rank and unfamilar odors did not tempt her, even though she was becoming more hungry by the minute.

Then Margit came to buildings with almost no windows at all. Carts and wagons were being loaded and unloaded in front of them. Huge, muscular, dark-haired and dark-skinned men stared at her curiously. Margit turned and fled in the direction from which she had come. Again she found herself passing shops, and there were some women and children on the walks. She kept going and hours passed but nothing seemed familiar.

The sun had begun to drop toward the horizon. Margit was so weak from weariness and lack of food that every step required effort. She must keep moving, but where was she going?

If only she could ask someone how she could get to Mrs. Bronson Smith's house, but no one on the streets of New York City could understand or speak Norwegian. Even if they could, how would they be able to direct her to Mrs.

Smith's house? It was inconceivable that everyone in this great city knew everyone else, as they did at home in the parish of Tysvaer.

She had certainly blundered into a terrible situation. It would be dark soon and then what would she do? It wasn't only her stomach that ached now. Her chest and throat and head and eyes—not to mention her feet—felt as though something terrible was happening to them.

After all, an orphan had no business leaving Norway in the first place, without being directed to a responsible person who would take charge of her. But if she came to a bad end, she would have only herself to blame.

Margit was so absorbed in self-denunciation that she had stopped paying attention to her surroundings. But suddenly she found herself in front of a church, whose high spires towered above even the tallest buildings. This section of the city was entirely different from anything she had seen in her wanderings, and, tired as Margit was, her curiosity prompted her to pause to examine the place. From its appearance, this must be a very important church. Margit turned the corner and walked along the side of it. It was surrounded by a well-kept churchyard, with rows of old tombstones. She went on, but there were no buildings beyond the churchyard, which sloped down to a river. Could this be the great Hudson of which Master Cleng had talked so much? The lonely spot gave Margit an eerie feeling, and turning quickly around, she walked back to the church.

For a moment Margit stood on the corner, not sure which direction to take. A narrow street to her right looked interesting and she decided to try that. Once more she passed elegant houses set well back from the sidewalk. But now and then, among them, were fashionable-looking shops. It was easy to see that this was a neighborhood of aristocracy and wealth and that the street itself was an important one. This place corresponded exactly with the description of the site which Ann Jensen and her husband from Bergen originally farmed. This fine street must be the great Wall Street, of which Master Cleng had so often spoken, and the church, the famous Trinity Church. The fabulous tales he had told about the place came back to Margit. She recalled the enormous fortunes of everyone. So wealthy were they, he had boasted, that silver American dollars rolled down the cobblestones of the street. Margit bent down and examined the pavement, but sharp-eyed as she was, she was unable to spot a single silver coin.

Disappointed, she again became conscious of how tired she was. The gathering darkness frightened her. She started to run, blindly covering the distance until she was again among crowds of people, where there was more traffic in the street.

Margit noticed a man standing on the corner with his arms folded. He looked important, even though he was not wearing the uniform of a government official. She decided to go up to him and try to make him understand her alarming situation.

"My name is Margit," Margit said in Norwegian. "And I am lost."

The man said something, too, apparently in English, and all Margit understood was the repetition of her own name.

"I have just come from Norway and I am lost," Margit said.

The man shook his head.

"I came from Norway on the ship called the *Restoration*," Margit said. "But I am an orphan and have lost my way."

Still the man stood regarding Margit, a puzzled expression on his face.

"I came from Norway on the *Restoration*," Margit said, speaking very slowly.

A look of understanding seemed to be coming slowly into the man's face. Margit was quick to notice it.

"I came from Norway on the *Restoration*," she repeated. The man nodded his head. It was evident that something had come through to him. He took Margit's arm and started walking as if he knew exactly where to go. Although she was fearful of being piloted in the gathering darkness by this perfect stranger, it seemed her only chance of ever again getting in touch with her fellow passengers of the *Restoration*, and, most important of all, with Master Cleng. The prospect of being forever separated from him in this strange land was enough to make her risk anything.

As Margit tried to keep up with the stranger's long, rapid strides, she found herself now running breathlessly beside him, now tagging a few steps behind with her eyes fixed on his broad back. An overcast sky added to the darkness of the oncoming evening. This would remain in Margit's memory as the longest and the most terrible walk in all her life, but finally they reached a body of water. They walked along the water front for some distance, and then the stranger stopped at one of the piers. By now it was completely dark, but suddenly Margit recognized the Norwegian flag floating above a kerosene lamp high on the *Restoration*'s mast. Never had her flag—the blue and white cross against its red background—looked so beautiful to Margit, as it fluttered in the gentle breeze.

"Thank You, God," Margit whispered. This prayer, too, like the one she had uttered during the storm at sea, rose instinctively to her lips.

Captain Helland and Mate Erickson were out on deck. The stranger spoke a few words with Captain Helland. Then he shook hands with him and left.

Captain Helland looked stern in the light of his kerosene

lantern as he spoke to Margit. "Don't you know better than to wander off alone in this huge, strange city?" he asked, his tone even more severe than his look. "It was your good fortune to have come in contact with this official of the law, and to have stumbled upon the idea of repeating 'Norway' and the '*Restoration*,' which are pronounced almost the same in Norwegian as in English. Otherwise, I tremble to think of what might have happened to you."

Margit hung her head.

"Cleng Peerson is going to be furious when he learns of this," Erickson said. "Haven't you caused him enough worry by coming aboard as a stowaway, without getting him and yourself into still more trouble?"

Margit was too ashamed and too exhausted to speak.

"Let me check the passenger list to see where she is supposed to be staying," Captain Helland said. "Then one of us will have to take her back where she belongs."

Margit shifted uneasily from one foot to the other.

After consulting a paper from his pocket, Captain Helland said, "She has been billeted with a Mrs. Bronson Smith. I have her address. Do you think you could find the place, Erickson? It is quite a distance from here."

The two spoke softly together for a few minutes.

"We'll have to hire a carriage to take you to Mrs. Smith's," Captain Helland said. "How in the world did you get here on foot?"

"I'll go along with her," Erickson said. "Cleng Peerson has enough worries these days without this youngster getting out of hand once more. I'll manage to get back to the ship somehow. Perhaps Peerson will pay us back the price of the fare. He says friends are helping with the passengers' expenses during their stay in New York City."

On the ride from the *Restoration* to Mrs. Smith's home,

not a word was exchanged between Margit and Erickson. It was a long ride and, for Margit, a very painful one.

Mrs. Smith was out on the porch when the carriage arrived. There were lights in every window from attic to cellar. Without a word, the tiny lady helped Margit down from the carriage and led her into the house. The table in the dining room was set, as if guests were expected. It was only a matter of minutes before Mrs. Smith had Margit seated and was serving her hot, delicious food. Quite heedless of her manners, Margit attacked the food as if she hadn't eaten for days.

When Margit had finished her meal, Mrs. Smith pinned a piece of paper on Margit's dress. Twisting it right side up, Margit made out Mrs. Bronson Smith's name and some numbers. There were some words below that she could not read. Mrs. Smith made it clear that Margit was to wear this slip of paper as long as she stayed in New York City.

The warm welcome, the delicious food and the cheerful atmosphere in Mrs. Smith's house completely restored Margit's spirits. With the assurance that she would never become stranded again, her recent experience lost much of its fearful aspect. After all, she had learned a great deal today, which she would have missed if she had remained sitting on the front porch. In the future, however, she would be careful not to go too far when she ventured forth. In spite of everything, she certainly intended to see much more of this wonderful city before she had to leave it.

CHAPTER TEN

Although she was tired and sleepy the morning after her escapade, Margit was up early. She ate her breakfast hastily, for she wanted to be ready for Master Cleng when he came to give her the scolding which she expected and knew she deserved. She went out on the porch and waited for him with mixed feelings of dread and anticipation. For in spite of the unpleasantness she expected, she longed to see Master Cleng. It was not easy to find herself suddenly cut off from everything and everyone that had belonged to her old life.

Noon and afternoon and evening went by and still Master Cleng failed to put in an appearance. The next day, Margit again awaited him at an early hour, but that day passed, too, and he did not come. Margit grew increasingly anxious. He must have been even more angry with her than she had believed, and this new escapade of hers the very day following her arrival had undoubtedly not helped matters. Certainly Captain Helland and Erickson would not have minced matters in reporting to him for both men, she knew, had been thoroughly disgusted with her. One day rain fell in torrents, driven by a biting wind. Mrs. Smith came out on the porch, drew Margit into the house and put her on a chair beside the kitchen stove. For a little while Margit was content to sit toasting herself, but soon the boredom became too much for her. Sitting inside, she did not even have the activities of the street to distract her from her worries. She would have to do something to help pass the time or she would lose her mind.

Suddenly she had an idea. She pointed to the canary. Mrs. Smith looked bewildered. Margit kept pointing. Mrs. Smith said something Margit did not understand. She kept pointing, and after several repetitions of Mrs. Smith's sentences, Margit singled out the word *canary*. She repeated the word. A look of understanding lit up Mrs. Smith's eyes. "Bird," she said. Margit repeated the word *bird*. Mrs. Smith beamed. The language lesson was under way.

At first Mrs. Smith concentrated on her canary and her two white cats. *Feathers, wings, fur, paws.* Margit saw her mistake. Mrs. Smith's whole life was bound up in her three pets, and she took for granted that, since Margit had pointed to the canary, they were of prime interest to her as well. Margit did not expect to have use for an extensive vocabulary for either the canary or the two cats, but she did want to learn English words that would help her in daily living in America. So, during the noon meal, she pointed to her cup and saucer and looked inquiringly at Mrs. Smith. "Cup," Mrs. Smith said. In quick succession, Margit learned to say cup, saucer, plate, knife, fork, spoon, bread, butter, tea, coffee, milk, water. At the end of the rainy day, Margit was well on her way to learning English.

Sunshine and warmer weather brought Margit to her post on the porch again. Now her thinking was divided. She worried about Master Cleng, but she also strained her mind to the limit, trying to remember every word she had learned. At meals, Mrs. Smith obligingly cooperated with Margit in increasing her vocabulary. By the next day when Margit sat on the porch, she had a whole new list of words to add to those she already knew. She tried forming simple sentences. "Bread is good." "Sugar is sweet." "Water is cold." At times, Margit fretted over wasting the opportunity of seeing more of New York City, but she had to content herself with the knowledge that she was learning to speak English. She didn't dare to leave the house for even the shortest walk, for fear of missing Master Cleng, if he happened to come.

Finally, late one afternoon, Margit recognized his familiar figure coming down the street. He walked with long strides as was his wont, and he was carrying his walking stick.

Margit ran down the sidewalk to meet him.

"I'm sorry I caused you all that worry," Margit blurted out.

"I've been bogged down with worries these days," Master Cleng said gravely. "My biggest one, however, has been keeping Captain Helland and some of the others out of prison and trying to prevent the American customs officials from confiscating the *Restoration*."

"Are the officials such terrible people?" Margit gasped, horrified at what she had heard.

"Of course not. They are only carrying out the law. The plan was to sell the vessel as soon as it docked in the port of New York. My good Quaker friend, Francis Thompson, had warned against trying to dispose of too large a ship, and I wrote this to Lars Larson. But it seems that the Norwegian idea of a small vessel differs considerably from that of the Americans, and hence all the difficulty."

"How terrible for you to be having so much trouble," Margit said with real concern in her voice.

"And you have certainly not helped to make things any easier for me," Master Cleng said severely.

"Couldn't you explain to the officials that no one was to

blame for my being aboard the *Restoration?*" Margit asked. "I mean no one except me?" She was on the verge of tears.

Master Cleng's face softened. "Your being aboard made very little difference. It will take more explanation than that to settle the matter. Francis Thompson and Larson expect to go to Washington and call upon President John Quincy Adams, and we hope they will be able to straighten things out satisfactorily. You see, the customs officials were absolutely dumfounded that you people had made the voyage in what they termed an "eggshell" and arrived safely in America. They said that the English *Mayflower*, which was four times the size of the *Restoration* and carried only half as many passengers, was considered far too small to make the voyage across the ocean."

After having recovered from her initial fear that she had been the cause of additional worry to Master Cleng, Margit was greatly relieved at the turn the conversation had taken. It was giving her time to prepare for the scolding from Master Cleng about her escapade in New York City.

By this time they had reached the porch and when they were both seated on the steps Master Cleng said, "I heard you have itching feet."

"Yes, but I didn't intend to go so far, Master Cleng. I only wanted to see a little of New York and—and—and I walked—"

"And you kept walking—"

His tone wasn't nearly as stern as Margit had expected. "It was all the fault of these Norwegian boots of mine, Master Cleng. When I tried to make them retrace my steps, they just—"

"Wouldn't obey and brought you instead to a stranger with whom you proceeded to walk down to the water front."

"But he was an official. Captain Helland told me."

"Your luck, not your common sense, sent you to him."

Margit looked up at Master Cleng. "Are you really very angry with me, Master Cleng?"

"If you'll promise me never to start out on such a fool-hardy jaunt again, I'll forgive you this time."

Margit could have wept for joy.

"But I really came," Master Cleng continued, "to tell you that we are starting out in the morning for the site of our colony."

Again Margit's spirits fell.

"Will—will—will you go with the others?"

"Of course. I'm especially pleased that we shall be taking one of the new steamers that make the trip between New York and Albany."

Margit bit her lip, and stared at her feet.

"Aren't you pleased? Don't you want to go with the others?"

"If you had only let me know earlier, Master Cleng, I could have earned the money."

Master Cleng chuckled. "Our very good Quaker friends are paying for everyone's passage."

Margit looked at Master Cleng inquiringly.

"They are so thankful for what America has meant to them that they are extending a helping hand." Then Master Cleng's expression became grave once more. "But don't get the idea that one expects other people to help continuously even in America. It is because people here have made use of their opportunities that they have become prosperous." Then he rose from the step. "Now I must be going. There are still things to be done. Be ready early in the morning when we come for you. Before I leave, however, I am going in to thank Mrs. Bronson Smith. I see she has done very well by you."

After Master Cleng had left, Margit thought about their conversation. It was wonderful how a person in America could manage to overcome any sort of difficulty. On the other hand, there seemed to be so many more difficulties here than in Norway that a person could blunder into, if he wasn't careful. Well, she for one intended to be on her best behavior from now on. The first thing would be to be ready to leave with the group in the morning. It was going to be a wonderful experience—traveling up the Hudson River in one of those newly invented steamers she had heard so much about, and then going overland and seeing more of this great country.

The following morning when it came time to leave Mrs. Smith, Margit felt almost sorry. The two white cats, with gentle urging from Mrs. Smith, each put out a paw as a gesture of good-by. The canary, needing no encouragement, trilled its farewell with amazing eloquence. Mrs. Smith, holding Margit's hand in one of hers, and the bundle of clothing she had made up for her in the other, patted Margit lightly on the cheek. The carriage which had come for her was the finest in which Margit had ever ridden. But she waved to Mrs. Smith as long as her house remained in sight before she sat back to enjoy this elegant passage through the crowded streets.

At the pier on the Hudson River she could scarcely believe her eyes when, with the other passengers from the *Restoration*, she was taken aboard the shining new vessel. When she found herself on deck sitting with strangers as well as the Norwegians she knew, the wonder of this new experience overwhelmed her. Back in Norway Master Cleng had sung to her about the great ancient Viking ship *Ormen Lange*. But this ship she was on was much more interesting than that one could possibly have been. For without benefit of sails or oars, but with only its side-wheel paddles, it was moving swiftly and steadily upstream in the middle of the great river.

As the water divided, she looked up and saw that the ship was leaving a trail of black smoke, a giant replica of the puffs that old Jonas, back in Mistress Catherine's kitchen, used to send forth from his long-stemmed brown pipe.

Margit watched the shifting scene on both sides of the steamer. So great was the ship's speed that the landscape on each bank changed continuously, revealing the most amazing sights. There were huge forests, different from any she had ever seen in Norway. They extended over almost entirely level ground or along the top of high palisades. Many of the trees were covered with brightly colored leaves. In places the forest gave way to tremendous fields with brown and yellow stubble giving evidence of bountiful harvests. Some of the fields had already been plowed, ready for new seeding, and the rich black loam that had been turned contrasted with the vivid coloring that surrounded it.

It must be wonderful to be living in the huge, white country homes that appeared in quick succession along the river bank, Margit thought. Each was in the center of a cluster of red and white smaller buildings, any of which seemed fit for human habitation. Bushes and trees and gardens with flowers still in bloom gave witness of loving care by those who occupied these fine houses. Would the passengers of the *Restoration* ever be blessed with such luxury? Margit wondered.

She had been so absorbed in what she was seeing that she had not noticed Master Cleng who had come over to stand beside her. As she turned to look at the opposite bank of the river, she saw him, and smiled.

"I take it you are enjoying the trip up the river," he said.

"America is a great land," she breathed.

Master Cleng went over to a smokestack and carried a bench toward the front of the boat. Margit followed him.

"There, that's better," he said as the two sat down. "All our passengers seem to be fairly well settled now, so I can relax a bit."

Margit was too happy to speak. Master Cleng had left all the other passengers and had come to sit beside her. Now he seemed more like the Master Cleng she had known in Norway. She would dare to talk to him now, just as she had in those days.

"Master Cleng," Margit began, "did you organize this colony in America so people from Norway could get rich and own beautiful homes?"

Cleng Peerson threw back his head and laughed heartily. "You have certainly been listening well to what people have been saying."

"Will they find American silver dollars rolling along the ground or growing on trees?" Margit asked.

"Those tales sound fantastic enough," Master Cleng admitted. "I dare say the truth has been colored up a bit. Yet," and the smile left his face, "you will live to see many of these miracles actually happen."

"I've already seen some," Margit said enthusiastically. "Every time I turn around, something I never dreamed of appears or happens. Oh, Master Cleng, America is a wonderful country!"

Master Cleng patted her shoulder. "So speaks the true American pioneer," he said approvingly.

Margit repeated her first question for it was uppermost in her mind. "Master Cleng, you were wonderful to plan all this for the passengers of the *Restoration*, but *was* it just so they could get rich and own beautiful homes?"

"No," Master Cleng said. He adjusted his body into a more comfortable position on the bench and crossed his legs, just as he used to do back in Norway when he was about to tell Margit and Ingrid a tale he considered of utmost importance.

Then he cleared his thoat and began, "It all goes back to about ten or eleven years ago when Norway was forced into a war against England. Many of our men were called upon to fight and some were taken aboard an English prison ship. During their imprisonment, an English Quaker missionary came and spoke to them. Our Norwegians were impressed with the earnest, simple faith of this man of God, and some of them were converted to his religious beliefs. When they came home, they were no longer willing to let the church officials of Norway do their thinking for them. They were Quakers now, but when they tried to hold meetings where they could worship as they believed was right, they were forbidden to do so by the Norwegian church officials. The officials also caused the men to lose their jobs and many of them had to struggle to make a living for their families.

"It isn't easy to live in a country where one is neither permitted to work according to one's abilities, nor to think for oneself, nor to worship according to one's conscience. But of the three hardships, Margit, the last one is the worst, for it upsets the pattern of one's entire life. In Norway, young couples who were married in the manner of the Quakers were declared by the church leaders to be living in sin, and their children were branded as illegitimate. Can you imagine what such a stigma, even though undeserved, might do to a fine family like the Lars Larsons?

"My heart went out to the Elias Tastads at the time of the death of their infant twin daughters. Because the Tastads insisted upon the Quaker funeral rites, they were banned from burying the babies in the parish churchyard, and the little coffins were placed in the Tastad garden. At this, the local church officials demanded that the graves be opened and the bodies removed to the churchyard where proper rites could be performed according to the State Church. It was only after the King of Sweden intervened, responding to an appeal from the Tastads, that the officials withdrew their demands."

Margit sat listening intently, but she could find no words to speak.

"Most of the trouble has arisen from the abuses of the local church and government officials, who enjoy exercising their power over their victims," Master Cleng continued. "When I dared to disagree with them and voiced my disgust with their tactics, I was barred from attendance at our local parish church."

All that Master Cleng had been telling Margit was a revelation to her. But this last surprised her most. In the eyes of Mistress Catherine, the church and government officials could do no wrong. How could Margit have lived in that household all these years without an inkling of the basic religious differences which existed between Mistress Catherine and her husband?

At last Margit found voice to ask, "Were all the passengers on the *Restoration* at odds with church and government officials?"

"Yes. That is something I want you to remember, Margit. This colony which we are about to establish will come into being because, first and foremost, every man and woman has come here in quest of freedom to work, freedom to think for himself and most important of all, freedom to worship according to his own conscience."

Master Cleng spoke with such emphasis that it startled Margit. "I'll remember," she said meekly.

Then Master Cleng began to speak in a quieter and calmer tone. "With conditions as they are in Norway at present, those who are on this steamer felt they could make no headway there. They all wanted so very much to get a fresh start in life, and America seemed to offer the best prospects. So a group from the Stavanger area got together to send me here to investigate the possibility of suitable land where they could settle. I finally found some of the most wonderful land I have ever seen, and we are on our way there now."

Margit wanted to ask more questions about the passengers, but Master Cleng did not give her the opportunity. "I walked all the way from New York City to Kendall Township where we are about to settle. It was a revealing experience to behold mile after mile of fine rolling country. You have no idea what it means to be able to stretch out your arms so freely. In Norway we were hemmed in by mountains. Here there is space. A man can breathe and move as he wishes without getting in the way of others. That is the story, Margit, of why I returned to Norway and urged my friends and my family to migrate."

"But Norwegians have come to America before now," Margit said. "Don't you remember all the people you told us about? Especially the women who had migrated and become very rich?"

"True," Master Cleng admitted. "Both men and women have come from Norway through the years and have done very well, just as I said. There has even been one other attempt to establish a permanent Norwegian colony. Those people, too, sought religious freedom, as we are doing now. But like the Lost Colony of the English on Roanoke Island in Virginia, our earlier Norwegian colony was not well enough organized and it became a lost colony, too. Only the name of Bergen County in New Jersey now remains to remind us of the unfortunate failure of those people who migrated from our own city of Bergen, Norway."

"Aren't you afraid of such a failure, too?" Margit asked. These flattering confidences from Master Cleng were making her feel more grown-up and more important by the minute.

"The colony we're about to establish at Kendall will not fail," Master Cleng spoke emphatically. "As I told you before, every man and woman is dedicated to seeking and obtaining freedom to work and think and worship as it seems right for him to do. On the practical side, I have found good land, which can be bought at a reasonable price with plenty of time to raise the money to pay for it. Entire families are migrating this time and they will work together. The Erie Canal has just been completed. It has become an important waterway between the cities of Troy and Buffalo, New York. This means that ships can now run from the Atlantic Ocean, up the Hudson River, through the Erie Canal and onward over the Great Lakes. Goods can be shipped from Europe and Africa by water far inland to the center of the United States."

Margit looked puzzled.

"You are too young to understand much of what I am telling you now. But some day you will realize what a golden opportunity it is for our people to be coming here, Margit."

"It's very interesting," Margit said stoutly. "And I love to have you tell about it, Master Cleng."

"But I haven't mentioned the most important reason why I am telling you all this. As I have already mentioned to you, our people in this colony want to be free to think and to worship, as their consciences dictate. But also free to forge ahead to become what they want to be. A cottager and his family will have just as much of a chance to make good here as the owner of the manor house on one of the largest estates in Norway. The humblest shoemaker in the parish may some-day become one of America's foremost citizens."

The more Master Cleng talked about the Kendall Colony, the more anxious Margit became to reach it. She felt as though she would like to jump off the boat and rush at top speed overland in order to get there more quickly to begin to make a great success of herself.

Finally the steamer began to slow down and head toward the riverbank where a row of piers bustled with activity. Margit had risen and made her way to the very front of the boat. They had traveled far into the interior of New York State, past forests and plains, fields and deserted stretches of marshland, and now here lay the city of Albany.

The boat had docked. Master Cleng gathered his group about him and they all started down the pier. As Margit watched him, striding quickly and confidently toward land, she thought of Moses leading the Israelites into the Promised Land. There could be no doubt about it. God must have revealed Himself to Master Cleng, just as He did to Moses. And as God did in the time of Moses, He must now be helping Master Cleng's people.

Margit suddenly stopped. She was beginning to think and talk exactly as Master Cleng had done in Norway for years. It was a good thing Mistress Catherine was not here to probe into her mind as she so often had and ridicule her for building fragile castles in the air. Margit had all at once become anxious to start doing her part to make the Kendall Colony a success. Nothing must stand in her way.

CHAPTER ELEVEN

There was much more luggage to be brought from the pier to the open space outside a huge warehouse in Albany than the passengers had had when they disembarked from the *Restoration*. A few had some money with which to buy necessities. Almost everyone had received gifts from Master Cleng's friends, which would stand them in good stead during the first months in the Kendall Colony. Finally all the luggage was piled high, ready to be loaded into the wagons.

Again Master Cleng called the group together, this time just outside the warehouse.

"I want you fathers and mothers to come up closer," Master Cleng said, raising his voice for all to hear, "so I can explain to you exactly how we intend to proceed overland."

Margit found herself at the fringe of the circle of people assembled around Master Cleng.

"The men for whose wagons I have asked for the trek will have to be notified of our arrival and told to come here. Some purchases will have to be made to tide us over until we reach our land. We think that the trip will take us from a week to ten days. Then there will be the stop on the way to file claim for our land. Those of you who can speak English must go where you will be most needed. I shall write out directions for some of you and you will be able to accomplish your errands by showing the slips of paper I give you."

Some of the parents turned apprehensively toward the children and the luggage.

Master Cleng nodded. "Yes, I have thought of them, too. The older children will care for the younger ones and watch the luggage whenever there are no grownups at hand." Then he turned to Margit. "I shall depend on you, Margit, to see that what I have directed to be done by the older children is carried out."

Margit gulped with disappointment. She had counted on slipping off by herself to see what this city of Albany was like. It seemed to be a much smaller place than New York City, and since it lay so far inland, there must be a great deal of interest here that would be different from the metropolis on the Atlantic seaboard. But she was now one of the colonists, so it was up to her to take hold, even though the actual site of the colony had not been reached. Besides, she wouldn't start out wrong by deliberately disobeying Master Cleng.

Margit took up her post beside the luggage. She was no longer able to hear what Master Cleng was saying, but she kept one eye on him, and soon she saw men and women leaving in groups of two and three. Then Master Cleng left, too. A few of the mothers of the smallest children returned to where the luggage was piled, and they sat on the chests, holding the very youngest ones in their laps. One child, whose parents had both left began to scream, and Margit had all she could do to quiet him.

A period of seemingly interminable waiting followed. Children became restless and fretful. One mother opened the chest she was sitting on and brought out bread which she and Margit broke into chunks to feed the children. This helped for awhile and some of the very young ones fell asleep either in the arms of their mothers, or on blankets which Margit spread on the ground. She gathered a few of the older ones around her and told them stories of why trees in America had leaves which turned from green to bright shades of red and yellow and gold during the autumn. She also explained to them why the boat on which they had traveled up the Hudson River was able to move without oars or paddles or sails. The children were fascinated when she translated Norwegian words into English and told them that soon they would be using those words as easily as they were now expressing themselves in Norwegian. Each country, she said, had a language of its own and, since they had lived in Norway and would from now on make America their home, they would be fortunate in having two languages. For some time, Margit was able to interest the children by making a game of their learning English words.

But eventually they tired of their language lesson. The older ones began teasing the younger ones and complete chaos seemed on the verge of breaking out, when Margit had a sudden inspiration. In a loud voice, she said she had saved the most wonderful story of all for them, one they would never forget. But there would have to be absolute quiet, if she were to tell it. With their curiosity aroused, order was restored. Then Margit asked them if they had noticed how the bright lights on the streets of New York made night seem like day. "Well," she concluded, "sometime all America is going to have so many such lamps on its streets and in its houses that people are not going to be able to tell whether it is night or day, it will be so brightly lighted everywhere."

They regarded Margit with wide-open eyes, as if she

had told them they would some day reach the moon. Margit was desperately trying to think of what she could do next to entertain them when—wonder of wonders—a long procession of large wagons moved toward them.

Master Cleng sat on the front seat of the first wagon beside a strange man. As soon as his wagon reached the warehouse, he jumped down and said something in English to the driver. Then he went back to each of the other wagons and did the same. After the last wagon had drawn up, Master Cleng began personally to direct the loading of each one. As Margit watched him, helpful, firm, seemingly everywhere at once, she was filled with pride. She had grown up in the home of this great man and, in many ways, was closer to him than anyone else, even though she had arrived in America without his consent.

Chests, bundles of bedding, clothing and food were systematically placed in wagon after wagon, and then people, generally in family groups, climbed in.

All but the last two wagons had been loaded when it came Margit's turn. She was assigned a place between two girls on a plank at the very back of one wagon. This, too, was a distinct disappointment, for she would have liked to have been in one of the head wagons in order to be closer to those who would control operations, so that she would know what was happening. But, after all, every wagon would be covering the same ground and that was really all that mattered.

As the wagon train passed through the city of Albany, Margit's head swiveled constantly from side to side. Fortunately all the wagons were open, so she was able to see a great deal. And there was little that Margit missed. Perhaps, she thought, after the colony had been well settled and she was a few years older, she might return to Albany, and then she could get a closer look at this fine American city.

Before long the houses were farther apart and there were no sidewalks. Then long stretches of woods bordered both sides of the road. These woods were fascinating, for now that the leaves were gone, they resembled gigantic brushes, the kind that in Norway were made up of branches for scrubbing floors and furniture and anything else that needed to be thoroughly cleaned. To be sure, there had been, here and there in Norway, a few trees which shed their leaves, but Margit had never seen whole forests of them before.

The farther the wagon train traveled, the larger grew the woods and the smaller grew the houses. The houses looked newer, too, and the trees larger and closer. Margit took deep breaths. There was a strange, tangy fragrance from these bare trees entirely foreign to her. Everywhere one went in Norway there was the strong scent of evergreens.

A gray squirrel with a very bushy tail ran across the road and was in danger of being run over. The squirrel seemed totally unaware of its close call and stood at the edge of the road and contemplated the passengers in the wagon. Margit wished she had a tidbit to offer it. It seemed so tame that it might have been lured to come closer, but the wagon rolled on and left the squirrel behind.

These woods, Margit thought, must be a real haven for wild animals. And she began to watch for them. There were more squirrels, a few rabbits and a doe with its fawn, and Margit thought she caught a glimpse of a big brown bear in the distance. But fearing she might frighten the younger children if she called their attention to the animals, especially the bear, she enjoyed her observations in silence.

The wagon just ahead of Margit's stopped. Margit jumped out and found that the entire wagon train had come to a standstill.

"The horses have to be fed and watered," the driver said.

The owners of the horses unhitched them and led them to a nearby stream. Women spread quilts on the ground and busied themselves feeding the children. Margit offered to help, but there was nothing for her to do. After she had gulped down her share of the food, she started for the woods on one side of the road.

"We'll be starting again before long," Master Cleng called out to her. "You mustn't keep us waiting, Margit."

Margit was startled. Master Cleng must have eyes in the back of his head, she thought.

It was fun walking on the soft carpet of dried leaves. She dug her feet into them and covered her shoes with them. Back in Norway, the farmers would have made a feast of these leaves for their cattle. Not a single leaf was allowed to go to waste on Mistress Catherine's estate.

In the fork of a low branch, Margit saw an empty bird's nest. At her touch, it came loose and she held it in the palm of her hand. She wondered what type of birds had occupied it the previous summer and raised their family in it. Now she was sorry that she had touched the nest. Perhaps those same birds intended to return to raise another family in it the following summer. But no, in America everything was new. No doubt the birds, too, would want a new nest. She was on the point of taking the nest back with her to the wagon, but she thought better of this. It might tempt some of the younger children—give them ideas of hunting for nests in the woods after they reached their destination.

For eight days the wagon train moved on from dawn to dusk. Each night the women made up beds in the wagon boxes and the passengers slept under the open sky. It was chilly, but huddled together as they were and dressed in all their clothes, they managed to keep reasonably warm. The caravan passed through town after town, each smaller than

Albany. At one of these, Master Cleng accompanied all of the men into a building and when they returned, it seemed that they were the owners of the land which Master Cleng had selected for them. This was amazing news, and Margit did not even try to understand the transaction. Back in Norway, people who owned land had inherited it from their parents and the families had lived on their places for generations. Mistress Catherine's first husband had left his estate to her, since there was no one else to whom it could go. Margit had often heard it whispered that Mistress Catherine had been most discerning when she had married this landowner.

"Do we have to stay in wagons all the rest of our lives?" Carrie Nelson's small boy asked.

"My no," Carrie Nelson assured him. "In only a very short while now we shall reach the beautiful house Uncle Cleng has built for us."

It was more than a little while. And it seemed longer than it really was, for the road became narrower and more bumpy. The houses appeared at only very rare intervals. The woods were denser and blacker. Finally there was only a trail which the driver of the first wagon followed.

It was already the end of the second day on this trail when the driver of Margit's wagon suddenly jerked his horses back, for those ahead had stopped without warning. All the passengers scrambled out of the wagons. The men, women and children all started to talk at once. The wagon train had come to the end of its journey. The colonists had finally reached their destination.

Suddenly the hubbub ceased. A single voice was coming from one of the first wagons. Master Cleng was praying. His words began to come out clearly. "Thy kingdom come, Thy will be done in earth, as it is in Heaven."

Master Cleng was praying aloud! In all the years she had lived on Mistress Catherine's estate, she had never heard him pray. Mistress Catherine had always taken over family devotions, whether Master Cleng happened to be present or not. In fact, Margit had the impression that Mistress Catherine had her reservations about Master Cleng's spiritual outlook.

Now he continued to the end of the prayer, speaking with great earnestness as though he were asking God personally for everything mentioned in the prayer. The first words Margit had heard came back to her. "Thy kingdom come, Thy will be done in earth as it is in Heaven." It seemed a good omen to have been greeted on her arrival at her new home by this petition.

When the prayer was ended, Margit stood beside the wagon in which she had traveled so far and she made a promise to herself. She would do everything she could to make this project, so dear to Master Cleng's heart, what he hoped and wished it to be.

CHAPTER TWELVE

When Margit woke up the next morning, she saw nothing but trees. Woods to the right of her, woods to the left, woods in front of her, and when she turned her head, there were woods behind her. She sniffed. There was the scent of evergreens and also the strong tangy smell of bare trees and fallen leaves, which she had learned to recognize during the trek up to Kendall from Albany.

Margit yawned and snuggled into the quilt which had kept her fairly comfortable all night, even though only a few evergreen boughs had separated her from the bare ground. The sky above her was a clear blue. It was going to be a beautiful day.

This was adventure. Robinson Crusoe's experiences on his deserted island were tame compared to this! Master Cleng had picked up a book about Crusoe on one of his travels and he had told Margit the story time and again. Margit remembered how he had translated many of the incidents word for word and Mistress Catherine had thoroughly disapproved, since to her there were only two books worth reading—the Bible and the church hymnal. It had been a source of comfort to her that *Robinson Crusoe* was written in a language which Margit could not read.

Noises in the distance and the tantalizing aroma of coffee brought Margit out of her daydreaming. She jumped up and, since she was fully dressed, she had only to fold her quilt and she was ready for the day.

There was a bright fire with kettles of coffee and steaming porridge hanging above it. Many of the settlers were already at breakfast.

"There's a basin on the stump over there and a pail of water," Carrie Nelson told Margit.

Margit used her petticoat for a towel and then returned to the fire.

"Can't I help?" she asked.

"Yes. The smallest children are eating over in the cabin with their mothers, but there are several children here who have no one to take care of their breakfasts," Carrie Nelson said.

Then, for the first time, Margit was aware that there was a clearing in the distance and in the center of this stood a log cabin. It had been so dark and she had been so sleepy that she had not seen anything of the landscape the night before.

It was fun serving the children their food—bowls of porridge sweetened with molasses.

"Brother Cleng will have his cow brought over from the Careys' today," Carrie Nelson said. "Then there will be milk for the very smallest ones."

By the time Margit was ready to eat, she was ravenously hungry. And never had she enjoyed her food as she did her molasses-sweetened porridge and hot black coffee that first morning in the settlement.

"But where are the wagons?" she asked suddenly.

"The drivers were anxious to return to Albany. We were

up at dawn to unload the baggage and they started back as soon as they had eaten breakfast."

"But—where is the baggage?" Margit asked.

Carrie Nelson smiled. "We couldn't risk leaving it outside for fear animals would get at it or a sudden rain might come up. It is all piled over in Brother Cleng's barn. The cow won't suffer from having no shelter for a few days."

Sounds of swinging axes and falling trees came from the nearby woods.

"What's that?" Margit asked Carrie Nelson.

"The men have started to cut down trees. Logs will have to be measured and sawed off and boards planed. The big problem now will be to get as many shelters built as possible before the cold weather sets in and there is danger of heavy snowstorms."

Margit drew a deep breath. Cut down trees. Measure and saw off logs. Plane boards. Build as many shelters as possible. All this sounded like building a new world. The Book of Genesis with God's six-day creation of the Universe could have been little more spectacular!

As far back as Margit could remember, she had never seen nor heard of the raising of a single building. On the rare occasions when any carpentering was done, it was to repair sagging steps, tighten leaky roofs or replace worn boards in a wall. The main house, the servants' quarters, the harness and shoemaker shop, the barns, the dairy and all the other outbuildings had stood in place just like the trees, the sun, the moon and the stars. And, confined as Margit had been in Mistress Catherine's kitchen, there had been no opportunity to see much of anything else. The church and the buildings of a few of the neighboring farms were just as much a part of the landscape as the buildings on Mistress Catherine's estate.

"What would you like to have me do now?" Margit asked.

"The coffee and porridge kettles will have to be thoroughly scoured," Carrie Nelson told her. "There are plenty of ashes, so you will have no difficulty getting them clean and bright. After that, perhaps you would like to come down to the brook with some of us to fetch drinking water for the men. It's hard work felling trees."

Scouring pots and kettles was one of the tasks Margit had disliked most in Mistress Catherine's kitchen. She could still see Gunda, bleary-eyed from the smoke of the open fire, supervising the job and pointing out the slightest blemish if the job were not done perfectly. Now Margit scrubbed the kettles as though her very life depended on the outcome, and when she had finished they might all have served as mirrors to the most exacting housekeeper.

It was even more fun fetching water from the brook and taking it to the men who were felling trees. Already many had been brought down and some of the men were cutting off branches, some were measuring the trunks and a few had already started sawing off the logs. There was the sound of laughter and banter and Cornelius Nelson was singing a gay Norwegian song. Margit would have liked to have an ax or a saw and join the crew. Instead she contented herself with carrying branches over to the place where the fire had been built and breaking them so they could be used as kindling and firewood.

Fortunately the weather remained mild for the time of year, and day after day the sun shone and dried the firewood and logs.

"God is with us," Carrie Nelson said. "Brother Cleng says that in a week or two more, there will not only be a community house for the settlers, but also a few cabins for individual families."

Most of the cooking was done out in the open, for the stove in Master Cleng's cabin was only big enough to be used by mothers with very small children. Margit helped prepare and serve food to the men and the older children. She continued to scour kettles that grew black with soot from hanging over the open fire. But she was happiest when she could go into the woods and make herself useful to the men who were at work there. This gave her a sense of freedom she had never enjoyed before in all her life.

The morning set for building the community living house dawned crisp and clear. Everyone was astir early, and except for the smaller children and their mothers who still occupied Master Cleng's cabin, the entire colony assembled around the fire for breakfast. Spirits were high and there was much talking and laughter. Margit was too excited to eat. Besides, bowls of porridge had to be refilled and hot coffee served.

Master Cleng seemed to be everywhere at once. "In Norway, people boast about spinning and weaving and sewing a shirt in one day," he said. "We will show the Norwegians that in America, an entire building can be put up in the same time."

After the meal was finished, Margit watched him walking with great strides toward the spot where the community house was to be erected. As usual he wore his long black cloak, his fur cap and his high boots. As usual, too, he carried his walking stick, but instead of using it to steady himself over the stump-dotted ground, he waved it vigorously in the air, as if to emphasize the importance of the task which was to be performed. He turned around to make sure that the men who were to work with him were following him, and Margit caught sight of his sideburns, which had grown amazingly long, fluttering in the breeze.

There were bowls and cups and spoons to be washed and

pots and kettles to be scoured, and Margit had no intention of neglecting these chores which she had taken upon herself. But this morning she performed them with lightning speed for she didn't want to miss the slightest detail of this amazing construction feat.

The men were all gathered around Master Cleng when Margit arrived. A space had been cleared of stumps, leaves and underbrush, and the bare black earth had been leveled off smoothly. Long narrow sticks had been placed end to end to form a perfect rectangle, indicating exactly where the structure was to stand.

"Now you all know exactly what your tasks are to be," Master Cleng was telling the men. "Those of you who are to lay the foundation logs will get into operation first. Then those who are in charge of delivering the logs to the builders will be ready to supply them as they are needed. Those of you who will do the actual building must exercise great care, so that the structure will turn out as tight and firm as possible. I shall, of course, be on hand to oversee every step."

For a while Margit stood rooted to the spot as she watched the men get into action. As if by magic, a sturdy foundation gave real shape to the building. A vacant space in the middle of one side indicated where the door was to be. The high poles rose at the four corners of the rectangle. In her imagination Margit began to see what the house was to be like.

"Go up to my cabin and fetch the keg of nails," Master Cleng told her.

Margit was startled. She had been completely absorbed in the activity, and she had not thought that Master Cleng, so intent on what he was doing, was even aware of her presence.

Without stopping to answer, Margit rushed off. As she ran, she realized that standing wide-eyed, watching others work, was not going to contribute anything to the building of the community house or to the settlement of the colony.

Inside Master Cleng's cabin, mothers were busy feeding and changing their children, washing clothes and preparing food that would be brought out to the men. It was warm in the cabin, and for the first time Margit caught sight of the American stove that everyone had been discussing. She would have liked to examine it and see how it worked, for there was not the slightest trace of smoke in the cabin, but she realized that Master Cleng would be impatient with any delay and she had already dawdled enough for one day. A layer of logs had been laid on top of the foundation when she returned to the building.

"Good girl," Master Cleng said, relieving her of the nails. "And now, if you will be so kind, we'd appreciate a drink of fresh water."

Carrie Nelson had also arrived on the scene, and she and Margit started out for the brook, each carrying a pail.

All day Margit ran errands. Food and water had to be served on the spot, in order to cut to a minimum the time the men took off from their work. Margit carried logs from a nearby pile. After the men were perched high on the walls and finally upon the roof, she mounted a stump and handed them nails and tools.

The pounding of hammers and the swinging of hatchets were music to Margit's ears. Every stroke meant progress. Every nail that was pounded into place meant that the building was nearing completion. This was real living. If an entire house could be built in a single day, what could be expected in a single year? In two years? In five?

When the walls and the roof had been finished, Margit stepped inside. There was space for a single window and for the door. The building, though small, was compact. It was not as large as Mistress Catherine's kitchen, but it would house a great many people, and it meant shelter and protection for them. As Margit stood inside and admired it, her heart was filled with pride and gratitude. Master Cleng had explained that after a community storehouse and a few other outbuildings had been taken care of, individual cabins would be built. Thus, gradually, there would be more space for those left in the community dwelling house.

Master Cleng did not trust anyone but himself to put in the window. Margit was sent up to his cabin to fetch this, too. She watched with bated breath as Master Cleng eased it into the enclosure which had been left for it. It fitted perfectly. How could Master Cleng have estimated the size of the hole so accurately and gotten four panes of glass in a frame long before there was any building at all?

As soon as he had finished putting in the window, he asked Margit to get warm water and a cloth from his cabin and wash the window. "The occupants of this house will want to see all the wonders that surround them," he said.

Margit rubbed the four panes of glass, both inside and out. When she had finished, Master Cleng came over to inspect. "That will do," he said.

Margit was a little disappointed that he had not been more generous with his praise. But by now he was busy with several of the men putting hinges on the door and hanging it up where it was to be attached to one side of the opening left for it.

"Why, Master Cleng, I didn't think you could make a door so fast!" Margit exclaimed.

Master Cleng looked up from his work and there was a twinkle in his eye. "In America, one says, 'Door, put in an appearance,' and presto, it comes all ready to be hung, hinges, latch and all."

Margit's mouth fell open.

"Brother Cleng, this is too much, even from you," Carrie Nelson, who had been standing close by, remonstrated. "He did do a quick job of it out in the woods, Margit, while he was overseeing the felling of trees and cutting of logs and planing of boards. But his boasting is getting a little out of hand when he would have you believe that the door appeared out of thin air."

"Maybe I did use my imagination a little too freely," Master Cleng admitted. "But you'll have to agree, Carrie, the appearance of a ready-made door out of thin air, as you say, is no more fantastic than your superstition that Christmas elves come to eat the cream pudding set out for them and so bring good luck for the coming year. And tossing salt over your left shoulder and—"

"That's entirely different," Carrie Nelson interrupted him. "Now don't you go and disillusion the child about important beliefs."

It was getting dark when it came time to lay the floor. Wonder of wonders, Master Cleng produced a kerosene lantern by which the men could see to work. Supports had been laid on the ground and two rows of rough, stanch planks nailed crosswise over them at one end of the room, when Carrie Nelson asked Margit to help serve the evening meal. It would be one of the last meals served out of doors. Master Cleng planned to accompany several of the men into the city of Rochester in the morning to buy a stove similar to the one in his cabin for the community house. It might take a day or two to install it, but before long all the cooking in the colony would be done in true American fashion on a truly American stove.

It was late in the evening before the meal was over and dishes and food had been cleared away. Still later, the last

nail was pounded into the flooring, and Master Cleng announced that the community living house was finished and
was ready to be occupied. Some of the younger children were
already asleep and had to be carried into the house. But no
one objected to helping them inside. Margit, herself, made
many trips between the open fire outside and the new house,
laying her burden down carefully either in a bunk or on the
floor beside other sleepers.

When there was nothing more for her to do, she returned
to the fire. There was still warmth from it and she sat down
on a chunk of wood close by and thought over the day's
happenings. It had certainly been an eventful day, one she
would never forget—not even if she lived to be a hundred
years old.

CHAPTER THIRTEEN

For weeks there had been only one thought in the minds of the people in the Kendall Colony—the celebration of Christmas. The holiday season, which in Norway had always been the high point of the year, lasting thirteen days, had made a break in the long winter and brought hope and cheer into the humblest cottager's home. To the new Americans, it meant a renewal of home ties and something to look forward to after weeks of backbreaking labor. Everyone had worked hard to accomplish all that had to be done. Now young and old looked forward with equally enthusiastic anticipation to the great event. The festive meal on Christmas Eve would be a welcome change from the usual porridge, black coffee, potatoes and carrots and, on rare occasions, a taste of meat or fish. And it would, of course, be the highlight of the celebration.

To Margit, Christmas meant much more than good food. There had always been plenty of that at Mistress Catherine's —especially for festive occasions. But the holiday preparations had also entailed extra hours in the kitchen, so that by the time the Holy Eve arrived, she had almost forgotten what the world outside looked like.

Here in the colony, during all the Christmas preparations, she had been free as a bird. She had gone out with the fishermen and had stood outside the community house skinning and scaling fish and getting them ready to be brought into the storehouse where they would be frozen for future use. She had even gone out in the woods with the hunters on one eventful day and watched one of the men bag a deer. Always she was on the move. She knew what was happening down in Master Cleng's cottage, where some of the mothers and their small children still lived. As for the community house, crowded to utmost capacity, it was always teeming with life and excitement. She knew about the mittens and scarfs and socks mothers and sisters and wives were knitting in secret—a major accomplishment under the circumstances— for their loved ones. She watched the men out in the cold and sometimes under the cover of darkness, making tables and chairs and stools which were to be not just Christmas presents, but the first furniture for the homes which were to be built before too long. She kept confidences. She ran errands. She helped with the baking and cooking, too, but only for short periods at a time. The capable housewives preferred to do most of the work themselves and entrusted to her only such jobs as stirring and mixing, turning flat bread after it had been placed on top of the stove to bake, and washing pots and pans. All in all, Margit had been so buoyed up for weeks with the Christmas spirit that if it were not now the twenty-third of December, with the climax only a few hours away, she never would have been able to stand the suspense.

Master Cleng had asked her to join him at his cabin that morning. As she walked over the narrow, slippery path leading from the community house to his cabin, she hummed under her breath "*Silent Night, Holy Night.*" She thought of how all the cottagers and servants on Mistress Catherine's estate had always assembled in the manor house—the one occasion when Mistress Catherine permitted this—to hear the church bells down in the village ring in the Holy Eve and afterward to gather at the great feast. This had been a festive occasion, and the memories of the joyful faces and the good wishes of many of those she knew and loved gave Margit the first slight twinge of homesickness she had felt since she left Norway.

Margit's last two Christmases in Norway had been the happiest in her life because of Ingrid. Ingrid had given her presents—the first year a lamb carved out of bone and highly polished. The second Christmas Ingrid had given her a candle holder, also made out of polished bone, and a red candle, which Ingrid herself had made from tallow dyed with red root juice. Margit had missed Ingrid since her arrival in America, this morning especially. But after all, one couldn't have everything in this world.

Master Cleng was standing just outside the door of his cabin. "Did I keep you waiting?" Margit asked.

"No," Master Cleng told her. "I only came outside to take a good look at the weather. God has been so considerate these past few weeks, making it possible for us to get so much work done out of doors that I was trying to see if He would give us a sign of what He intends for us over the holidays."

"And did He?" Margit asked.

Master Cleng shook his head. "I guess He means for us to enjoy the sunshine He is sending today and let tomorrow take care of itself."

Carrie Nelson came out of the cabin, carrying a huge wooden bowl piled high with *rullepolser*, boiled and pressed, all ready for eating. "Here, Cleng. Put them up on the top shelf in the storehouse where nothing can get at them," she said. "And be sure to cover them well with this cloth."

"How can you doubt that your slightest desire is your American brother's command?" Master Cleng asked, his blue eyes gleaming with mischief. Then he added more seriously, "Is this all?"

"My, no. I also have a bowl of head cheese that is all ready for the table. It isn't quite as heavy as the *rullepolse*, so Margit can carry that."

Carrie Nelson went into the cabin and returned immediately with the other wooden bowl.

Master Cleng regarded both bowls with great satisfaction. "My dear sister," he said, "no finer Christmas fare was ever produced in the entire Kingdom of Norway."

"That's a pretty strong statement," Carrie Nelson said, smiling nevertheless. "Remember that we had almost nothing but wild game to put into the *rullepolse* and the head cheese."

"Which only means the meats will have an extra fine flavor, for what animals could give more choice meat than those which have roamed the virgin forests of this great country?"

"That may be a matter of taste," Carrie said.

"Anyway, dear Sister, whatever ingredients you have to work with will, prepared by your hands, turn out to be the most delicious dishes men's hearts could desire."

"How you can talk," Carrie Nelson said. "And now you had better start for the storehouse and get the meat safely under cover before anything happens to it."

"I'll be very careful not to spill any of the head cheese," Margit said, taking the huge bowl.

"This Christmas celebration is going to be a memorable occasion in the history of the Kendall Colony," Master Cleng promised. "Never have people worked so willingly and so joyfully."

Carrie Nelson returned inside the cabin, and Margit and Master Cleng started down the path leading to the community storehouse. Although it was extremely slippery under foot, they both arrived safely with their burdens intact.

Master Cleng set his bowl carefully down on the snow and produced a tremendous iron key from the pocket in his cloak. He inserted it into a massive iron lock and the heavy door of the storehouse swung open. Master Cleng picked up the bowl of *rullepolser* and Margit followed him inside.

The two were greeted by the inviting smell of various foods. Shelves covering every available inch of space on the four walls were full of bundles and covered containers.

"I had no idea—why—where did all this food come from?" Margit asked.

"Many hands working many hours with much good will can accomplish wonders," Master Cleng told her smilingly. "You see there is going to be quite a feast on Christmas Eve here in Kendall Colony." Then his face sobered. "We shall use only a small part of these supplies then of course. We have been storing food like the squirrels, in case winter snows and storms shut us in for any length of time. I should not be looking forward to Christmas with such an easy mind if we were not so well prepared. For I have heard that the winters here are often much more severe than they were back in Norway."

Margit stood silent. Ever since her arrival in America, she had been surprised to discover things about Master Cleng that she had never known before. In Norway Mistress Catherine was always the one to worry about material things. In fact, she always seemed to regard Master Cleng as a fleeting guest, who came home and left, telling fantastic tales with no basic truth to them, a person who entirely lacked a sense of reality.

"Look," he said, pointing to a pillar of round sheets of flat bread extending from floor to ceiling. "You never saw such a stack of flat bread in the *stabbur* of the most prosperous farmer in Stavanger district."

"It's wonderful," Margit breathed.

"We're even supplied with enough potatoes to last into spring, if we dole them out carefully," Master Cleng said. "The young boys I have sent to the nearest farmers have done well. By threshing grain, as they have been taught to do, they have also brought back enough flour, too, and carrots and onions. But I shouldn't be standing here, giving you an inventory of our supplies. Carrie will become impatient waiting for the sack of potatoes I promised to take her for the *lefse*. The women waited until today to bake that, so it would be fresh for the Christmas Eve feast."

In a corner of the storehouse, he lifted a board from the ground, revealing a huge pit. From this he took a sack filled with potatoes.

"Look at the bulge each potato makes," Master Cleng said. "It would take three or four long, thin Norwegian potatoes to make a single, round, average-sized American one. I've seen American potatoes so large that they had as much food in them as a dozen of those which grow in the rocky soil of Norway."

After Master Cleng had finished his errand he locked the storehouse and put the key in his pocket. He tried the latch twice to make sure that the door was locked and that no harm could come to their supplies.

Back at the cabin he delivered the potato sack to his sister. "With these fine potatoes, you should turn out better *lefse* than you have ever made in all your life," he teased.

"I've noticed through the years that you have managed to

swallow Norwegian *lefse* in considerable amounts without too much effort," Carrie Nelson told him.

"Are there any more orders which you ladies want carried out?" Master Cleng asked, a twinkle in his eyes.

"Plenty of them," Carrie Nelson told him. "Tomorrow morning this cabin must be cleared for everyone to take Christmas baths here. The bathing can continue throughout the day. Those who are waiting their turn, or have finished, can stay in the community house, if they are not busy elsewhere. You must see to it, Brother Cleng, that there is an ample supply of wood at all times to keep the fire going, both in this stove and the one in the community house. There will have to be enough water to refill the kettles so that there will be plenty of hot water for the bathing. We don't want anyone to catch a cold."

"It shall be done exactly according to your commands," Master Cleng said, removing his fur cap with a flourish and bowing low.

"This is no joking matter," Carrie Nelson said severely. "Can you never be serious, Brother Cleng?"

"I was never more serious in all my life," Master Cleng said, but he was smiling as he spoke.

"The last-minute cooking will be done tomorrow," Carrie Nelson said. "By afternoon the table setting will begin. Fortunately the bunks along the walls have made bedmaking on the floor less of a problem, so there will not have to be nearly as much commotion with the bedding before and after the feast."

"And what would you have us men do tomorrow in addition to supplying wood and water for the baths?" Master Cleng asked.

"Bring up supplies from the storehouse as they are needed. Bring in the planks for the table and benches and set them up.

And, after the meal is over, clear them out and set up the Christmas tree in the middle of the floor so that everyone can march around it during the Christmas carol singing."

"Everything shall be done according to your instructions, Madam," Master Cleng told her, again bowing deeply. "There shall not be a single hitch in your plans."

"You should see the Christmas tree they cut down," Margit said enthusiastically. "I never saw a more beautiful one in Norway. Master Cleng showed it to me when we were down in the storage house."

"Do you hear?" Master Cleng asked. "Margit is already catching the American spirit."

"If boasting is the trait you are referring to, Brother Cleng," Carrie Nelson said. "You were blessed with that long before you reached these shores." But there was a smile on her lips and no malice in her voice.

All that day Margit went back and forth between the community house and Master Cleng's cabin. She carried pails of water. She brought armfuls of wood to fill the wood boxes. She carried messages from the women in one house to those in the other. She changed and fed babies when their mothers were too busy to do it. She told stories to the older children. She stoked the stoves when the fires burned low. She turned sheets of *lefse* when an emergency arose among the bakers. She sampled all the delicacies that were being prepared so that when mealtime arrived she was too full to touch a bite. Never had she worked harder, and never had she been so happy, chiefly because everything she did was requested, not commanded of her. Each task lasted only a short time, then she was free—free to come and go without giving an account of herself. It was the most wonderful feeling in the world not to be shut within four walls of a gloomy kitchen where everything she did was under scrutiny.

After the evening meal was over, Margit helped to clear away the food and wash the dishes. She was so tired she had to drag herself through these chores. Once she caught herself · nodding while evening prayers were being said. Even the smaller children seemed unusually heavy as she laid them in their bunks and tucked them in for the night. She stumbled wearily while trying to make her own bed on the floor. But finally, she managed to stretch out and cover herself snugly. She heaved a deep sigh of sheer joy. She had been needed; she had been wanted; she had been appreciated. And now, with all the others in the colony, she would celebrate Christmas tomorrow evening as one of them. She was the most fortunate girl in all the world. She closed her eyes and almost immediately drifted into a deep sleep.

CHAPTER FOURTEEN

Margit sat up. Was she awake, or was it only a dream? It seemed to her that the entire community house was ablaze with light. Never had the candle or the kerosene lantern seemed so bright. It couldn't be daylight already. By now Margit was wide awake. The house was dark except for the outline of the frosted window against the white snow. It must have been only a dream.

But suddenly there as a flash of light so bright that every corner of the room was visible. This was no dream. What could it be? Before she could decide, the flash was followed by a deafening roar. Then there was a steady noise, as if something were pounding against the wall of the house.

The room was again in darkness, but Margit heard people around her beginning to stir. Children whimpered and there was a low murmuring of voices.

"Such peculiar weather," a man said aloud.

There were more bright flashes, more deafening roars and more raging wind pounding against the house.

"In America anything can happen." Someone again spoke out of the darkness. "Who ever heard of lightning and thunder during a snowstorm?"

But now there was a steady light from outside.

"What is that?" someone called out.

"It's only lightning," someone else answered.

"It can't be. Lightning, even in America, can't look like that."

A figure was silhouetted against the window and the door was suddenly thrown wide open.

"Oh, God, help us! It's the community storehouse. The storehouse is on fire! The lightning must have struck it."

Someone lit a sputtering candle. People began tumbling out of their bunks.

"Everyone who is able come out and help fight the fire!"

That was Master Cleng's voice coming from the open door. Men and women were tumbling over one another, trying to put on their clothes. Babies were crying and older children were screaming. Margit staggered up from her bed on the floor. She tied a shawl about her head and shoulders and started for the door.

"Stay and take care of the children, Margit." Mrs. Rossedahl was out of the door before Margit could protest.

Margit looked around the room, now fairly lit up by the fire outside. Only children too young to help fight the fire were left inside. There was no alternative. She couldn't leave them, for there was no telling what might happen to them if they were left to themselves. She would have to stay behind and look after them. A wave of anger burned inside her. Why did people always take advantage of an orphan? She had never watched a big fire in all her life. At the moment she could think of nothing she would rather do than join those who had already gone out to it. But no, here she was stuck with a bunch of howling youngsters, each one trying to outyell the other. Then Margit pulled herself together.

There was only one thing for her to do right now and that was to quiet the children.

First she closed the door firmly so that it could not blow open again. Then she stirred up the fire in the stove. The house was thoroughly chilled. If any of the children were sick, things would become even worse. And there was the Christmas celebration to think of.

Suddenly Margit's heart sank. If the storehouse burned down, there could be no Christmas celebration. But how could she be so silly as to give in to such fears? With so many people on hand to put out the fire, there could be no possible danger of such a calamity. If worst came to the worst and the building itself couldn't be saved, Master Cleng would surely arrange to rescue everything stored inside it.

Calmed by this comforting thought, Margit turned to the children. All the babies needed changing. Then she heated water, added a little milk and sugar and fed it to the smallest ones. "If the rest of you will be quiet," she told the older children, "so the younger ones can go to sleep, I'll tell you some wonderful stories."

It took at least an hour before the last little boy was fast asleep and the older children had calmed down. Breathless, but relieved, Margit brought all who were to listen to her into two of the bunks and covered them with quilts.

What should she tell them? Visions of the fire fighters out in the cold blacked out everything else in her mind. But she had promised the children and they were waiting. And delay would make them impatient. Then she remembered one of Master Cleng's stories.

"Once back in Norway there was a man," she began softly. "He was so stingy that when Christmas came and everyone in the parish put out a large bowl of cream pudding for the elves, this man forbade his wife to do it. The elves became so angry that they decided this selfish man needed to be punished." Gradually the children, one by one, soothed by the gentle flow of her voice, began to drop off to sleep. Margit continued. "So during the year that followed, nothing grew on the place. Many animals died." Margit stopped. There was deep breathing from both bunks. "Never again did that man deprive the elves of their Christmas treat." The last child had dropped off to sleep.

The stillness in the community house became eerie. Outside the wind blew against the walls, but only intermittently now. The light from the fire had gradually become dimmer, and this added to the loneliness of the place. Margit would have liked to slip out and find out how the fire fighters were getting along. But she did not dare to leave the children even for a few moments, lest something happen to them.

Suddenly Margit sat up straight on her stool. Then she got up and walked around the room. A terrible thought had occurred to her. Could it be that Mistress Catherine had been right when she said that people were supposed to live out their lives in the place where they were born? Had evil trolls followed Master Cleng and the passengers on the *Restoration* across the Atlantic Ocean from Norway to America? Were they all being punished for leaving their native land? Was it the trolls that had set fire to the storehouse and not the lightning? Master Cleng made light of stories of elves and trolls, even though he could and did tell hundreds of them himself. But even he, at the Christmas Eve feasts, had always refused to touch a single morsel of food until Mistress Catherine announced that the Christmas elves had had their holiday cream pudding. It seemed that the elves and trolls were more active at that time of year than any other, and, as far as Margit knew, no one in the Kendall Colony had yet thought to feed the birds or to give the Christmas elves and trolls their annual treat.

Margit blamed herself for having neglected to remind Master Cleng about the matter. Everyone else had been busy caring for family matters. She, alone, was foot-loose and should have taken it upon herself to see that this important part of the Christmas preparation was done. Well, she had learned a lesson tonight that she would never forget.

As the night wore on, Margit became more and more worried. Things must be going badly out there, or one of the mothers would have run in, if only for a moment, to see about the children. The weather was bitterly cold and growing colder. There was a sharp draft from around the door and a chill from the walls. Suppose some of the fire fighters should lose hands or feet from frostbite? Or be accidentally burned? Margit felt sick at heart.

Finally, after what had seemed an eternity, Margit made out the suggestion of a dark gray rectangle where the window was supposed to be. Morning was coming at last. Then she heard crunching footsteps on the hard snow just outside the door. She went over and opened it. Mrs. Rossedahl stumbled in. Her face was streaked with soot and wet with tears.

"How—how is the fire?" Margit managed to ask.

"It took everything," Mrs. Rossedahl sobbed. "The fire burned all the food we had to live on this winter. We were not able to save even a single potato."

Margit led Mrs. Rossedahl to the stool on which she had been sitting. Then she poured water from the kettle—it was still lukewarm—and washed the exhausted woman's hands and face and dried them carefully.

"I'll poke up the fire and in no time I'll have a kettle of coffee ready. You'll feel better after you've had some."

As Margit hurried to make the coffee, she kept an eye on

Mrs. Rossedahl, for she could see that the poor woman was completely overcome with fatigue, exposure and emotion.

Mrs. Rossedahl had been somewhat revived by the heat from the stove and several cups of hot coffee, when the door opened. It was Master Cleng. His face, like Mrs. Rossedahl's, was streaked with soot, but there were no tears. For a moment he stood, taking in the bunks along the wall, crowded with sleeping children, Mrs. Rossedahl, her face and hands clean, still sitting on the stool by the hot stove and sipping coffee, and Margit stoking the fire with a fresh supply of wood.

"Have you any extra coffee?" was all he said.

"A whole kettle full and lots of boiling water," Margit told him, "so I can make more."

"Good," Master Cleng said. "I'll take it over to Sister Carrie in the cabin. She is preparing a meal for us over there."

As soon as the door had closed behind him, Margit turned to Mrs. Rossedahl. "Are you sure that nothing from the store-house was saved?" she asked.

"As I told you, not even a potato," Mrs. Rossedahl answered.

Children began waking up and again Margit had her hands full, cooking and serving hot porridge and molasses, washing hands and faces and quieting little ones who cried for their parents.

It was some time later that the grownups, one by one, began returning to the community house. All showed the effects of loss of sleep and the terrible strain they had been under. But their hands and faces were clean and they had made some effort to look presentable.

Carrie Nelson was one of the last of the women to arrive. "Brother Cleng has told me how well you cared for the children during the night," she said. "And we all appreciated the hot coffee you sent over to the cabin. It helped very much."

Margit blushed with pleasure at the praise, especially since much of it had come from Master Cleng. He wasn't given to praise, kind as he was.

Then Margit remembered the Christmas Eve celebration which was to have taken place. "There isn't going to be any Christmas feast tonight, is there?" she asked.

Carrie Nelson looked surprised. "Christmas feast?" she asked. It was as though Margit mentioned something she had not heard of before.

"I know," Margit said sadly. "There just couldn't be a Christmas feast without any food. All I could find here was coarse meal for the porridge and molasses and a little sugar. I gave whatever milk there was to the smallest children during the night."

"Who says there is to be no Christmas feast?" Master Cleng had returned to the community house.

Carrie Nelson turned in his question. "You know very well that is out of the question," she said. "Oh, we have the stack of *lefse* we baked yesterday, which fortunately was not brought down to the storehouse, and a few potatoes and some other odds and ends. And that's all."

"The very reason for going at once to prepare for our celebration," Master Cleng said.

"I told my husband that the only thing for us to do now was to try by whatever means possible, to make our way back to New York. And perhaps here we might induce someone to let us get aboard a freighter and sail back to Norway. We'll start fishing, all we can, and pay for our passage that way in time."

Master Cleng burst into hearty laughter. "You have certainly done a lot of planning in a very short while," he said.

"There is no other way. We'll all starve, trying to stay the winter here," Carrie Nelson told him.

"We built a storehouse once and filled it with supplies," Master Cleng told her. "What has been accomplished once can be done again. But that is not the question now. It is the morning of Christmas Eve. We have only a few hours in which to get ready for our celebration."

"How?" Carrie Nelson asked shortly.

"It is merely a matter of organization. Some of the older boys and the men will hunt, some fish. I'll leave the housekeeping duties for you to oversee, Carrie."

"It's bitterly cold. How can the men and boys hunt and fish in this weather?" Carrie asked him.

"They needn't go far. The woods are full of game, and there is a stream nearby with thin ice that can be cut. They can catch all the fish we'll need for the meal."

"And what are my housekeeping duties to consist of, without any provisions?" Carrie Nelson asked.

"By the time you ladies have the Christmas baths finished, some of us will have returned with our catches."

Margit stood by silently while Master Cleng and Carrie Nelson gave their orders.

Margit held her breath, waiting for her assignment. If Carrie Nelson asked her to take charge of the children again for the day, how could she refuse? Yet she was so tired of being cooped up in the house while all the others were free to be out in the open, even if it was to fight the fire or hunt and fish and do other things equally strenuous.

Suddenly Master Cleng turned to her. "Margit," he said, "I have a favor to ask of you. There is so much to be done that I am going to need the help of all the men. I'm going to have to send some of the older boys out in the woods for a Christmas tree to replace the one that was burned. We'll be wanting an especially pretty one, you know, and I'm not sure I can depend upon them to make a good choice. Would you go with them and see that they do?"

Would she? Margit felt two hot, telltale tears run down her cheek, and then a broad smile spread over her face.

"Before you start out," Master Cleng cautioned, "be sure to bundle up well. The storm has died down, but it's still bitterly cold."

Margit found several of the older boys waiting for her outside. Among them, so tall that he towered above the rest, stood a stranger. Margit looked inquiringly from one to the other of the boys she knew.

"This is Rolf Nordland," one of the boys from the colony said. "He works over at the Carey farm. They saw the fire last night and managed to get through the storm to help." Rolf Nordland greeted Margit with a shy grin.

"He's worked a lot in the woods during the winter," another boy spoke up. "And he volunteered to stay long enongh to help us cut down the tree."

Margit would have liked to ask about the fire and learn more of the details, but Rolf said it was best to get started. Like Master Cleng, he evidently thought of what had to be done instead of what had happened.

The group passed the place where the storehouse once stood. Only a blotch of soot and charred shapeless things remained. Margit shuddered.

"It's a good thing the fire didn't spread to the woods," Rolf said. "That Cleng Peerson certainly is a fighter."

The boys took such long strides that it was difficult for Margit to keep up with them. When she began to fall behind, Rolf Nordland waited for her.

"We won't have to go much farther," he told her. "We

can be looking now. If you see a tree that seems a likely choice, we'll stop."

He spoke in Norwegian, but there was an unfamiliar ring to his speech, so Margit knew he had not grown up around Tysvaer.

After they had gone a little farther, Margit said, "I think that's a pretty tree over there."

"Come back, boys," Rolf called out.

He and Margit walked over to the tree she had pointed out. "It is rather tall," Margit said.

"That's easily remedied," Rolf said. "It has close, well-shaped branches, and I think it would make a good Christmas tree."

The other boys walked around the tree.

"What do you boys think?" Rolf asked.

"It's up to Margit," one of the boys said. "Cleng Peerson said she was to decide."

Rolf turned to Margit. "What do you say?"

Margit felt her cheeks burn. In all her life, she had never been shown such deference. "I—I think it will make a beautiful Christmas tree," she murmured.

As Rolf prepared to cut down the tree, Margit watched him. There was a strength about his appearance that made him seem a natural part of the landscape. He had the ruddy cheeks typical of someone who had been born and lived much of his life out of doors. He walked around the tree, measured distances by counting paces and finally leaned over and put his hand on one side of the trunk.

"We'll start cutting right here," he said. "Then, when it falls, it will come down between those two trees over there and won't harm either of them." He took out a knife and made several notches where his hand had been.

He's a real woodsman, Margit thought. As he directed the

felling of the tree, she became more and more curious about his background. Rolf Nordland was a nice name. And he worked at the Careys, but he didn't really belong there. Margit decided he had not lived long in America. Where had he lived in Norway? How did he happen to come to America? And up here so far away from New York City?

The boys took turns wielding the ax, while Rolf directed how the tree was to come down.

Once back in the house, there was so much work to be done if there were to be any Christmas celebration at all, that Margit had no time to think about Rolf Nordland's past. The fishermen and hunters returned and Margit helped them to get fish and meat ready for cooking. It was too cold to stand outside to clean the fish and dress the game, so the house had to be given an extra cleaning when these messy jobs were finished.

At last it was time for the planks to be brought in from the lean-to and set up as tables and benches. They had been thoroughly scrubbed for the occasion and Margit gave each table a festive look by placing a candle in the center and scattering tiny sprigs of evergreen along the boards.

At Mistress Catherine's, the church bells had ushered in the holiday season. But now, as the men, women and children quietly took their places, there were only the low greetings of *Glaedelig Jul* to remind them that this was Christmas Eve.

It was already late and the smaller children were so hungry and sleepy that Master Cleng suggested that the food be served before the devotions. There was enough *lefse* to go around, even though the piece each person received could not have been described as huge. Master Cleng insisted that the American potatoes out of which the *lefse* were made contained at least five times as much nourishment as those grown in any part of the world and had a flavor equaled by none.

Cornelius Nelson declared that if ever better and tastier fish swam in fresh or salt water, he would have none of them, for he was sure they would not be of this world. Several of the older boys said they preferred wild game to domestic meat. And when it came to the traditional Norwegian Christmas Eve pudding, Carrie Nelson explained that she had substituted milk for old-fashioned cream and that, with constant stirring, as far as she could make out, the pudding tonight turned out fluffier and had a more delicate flavor.

All during the meal, the children ate hungrily but in silence. When their portions were gone, they did not ask for more. But Margit noticed parents slip food from their plates onto those of their small sons and daughters, and even older brothers and sisters shared what had been given them with younger members of their families. The helpings of "cream" pudding were twice as large for the little ones as for the grownups. Margit saw one mother spoon all of hers into the mouth of the child on her lap. The coffee alone was reserved for the adults, and every cup of the hot, rather weak liquid, was drained to the last drop.

No one left the table hungry, but Margit knew, as did all the women and older girls, that Carrie Nelson had managed thriftily with the food she had to work with and that she had held back a good deal of it. And all the grownups were aware that whatever they could get along without tonight would help to ward off the threat of actual want tomorrow and the next day and the next.

When Master Cleng read the Christmas gospel, Margit sat spellbound. Was this exciting story, which Master Cleng read so dramatically, the same passage from the Bible Margit had listened to every Christmas Eve in Norway? She actually felt herself right with poor Joseph and Mary as they were turned away from the inn at Bethlehem and had to seek shelter for the night in the stable with the animals. She was so engrossed with the shepherds and their flocks that when Master Cleng pronounced the jubilant message of the angels, "Glory to God in the highest, and on earth, peace, good will toward men," she thought for a moment she had actually heard the rustle of the angels' wings. However, almost immediately she realized it had only been the branches of a nearby tree which the wind had brushed against the outside wall of the house.

Then Master Cleng closed the huge black leather Bible with its gilt trimmings and clasps. He folded his hands and bowed his head. "Let us pray," he began. "We come to Thee, dear God, to thank Thee for Thy great mercy in saving us from suffering and death during the night which has just passed. And for the shelter which we and our animals still enjoy. We also thank Thee for Thy great bounty, which has provided us this day with food, not only for this feast, but for days to come. Teach us to trust in Thee, that, as our days are, so will Thy help to us also be. Bless us who are assembled in our new home in this wonderful land. Remember our loved ones who are still back in Norway. All this we ask in the name of Thy Son and our Saviour, Jesus Christ."

Everyone breathed a grateful "Amen" at the end of the prayer. It was as though a great force had raised their spirits. Margit had never heard such fervent expressions of *"Tak for maten."*

With the tables and benches out of the way, the Christmas tree was brought in and set in the center of the room. Children and grownups joined hands and formed rings around the tree and the carol singing began. Master Cleng's voice, which could scarcely have been rated as that of an artist, rose above all the rest and he sang lustily verse after verse of every hymn. In fact, to Margit's surprise, his store of

Christmas songs seemed as inexhaustible as that of his stories. Long after the smaller children had been put into the bunks and were fast asleep and many an older person had sunk to the floor from sheer exhaustion, he continued, starting up one song as soon as the other had ended. Often, because the other singers either ran out of words or voice, he was left to carry on alone. But this did not dampen his ardor for singing, and he finished triumphantly pronouncing the last word of the last line with as much spirit as the first one. Finally Carrie Nelson declared that if she did not start out for her cabin at once, she would have to be carried there. Master Cleng admitted that a little rest might not be amiss for all of them, and even a few winks of sleep.

Margit alone felt no desire for either. She put on her coat and tied her wool scarf over her head and slipped out the door. The night was cold but clear, and there was no wind. A full moon looked down upon her and the deep-blue heavens were dotted with bright stars. The snow in its freshness seemed blue-white in the darkness.

Margit walked slowly away from the house. The words which Master Cleng had read came back to her, but it wasn't the actual story of the Christmas gospel which had intrigued her so much during the reading. It was the humbleness of Christ's surroundings as He lay in His manger that first Christmas night so long ago in Bethlehem. They were, in fact, more humble than the community house in which the members of the Kendall Colony had celebrated their first Christmas Eve in America. Yet that first Christmas Eve in Bethlehem was the most memorable of all. And Margit knew that she had caught the true significance of that first Christmas Eve tonight as she had never done before.

She had almost reached the spot where the storehouse had stood when she became aware of the figure of a man close beside it. He was on his knees in the snow. His hands were folded, but his head was turned toward the heavens and the stars. In the still, crisp air, Margit could hear his words. "Thank Thee, O God, for granting us this blessed Christmas Eve together tonight. That was all that really mattered. For Thou hast taught us by this experience, as never before, that if we put our trust in Thee, Thou wilt ever be mindful of Thy children here in the wilderness as in all other parts of the world."

It was Master Cleng. Margit did not wait to hear more. She turned around and, even though the soft mantle of snow would have silenced the sound of her footsteps, she tiptoed slowly back to the community house.

CHAPTER FIFTEEN

It was late January. Margit stood at a chopping block, trying to cut up a huge chunk of wood into sticks that would fit into the stove. The weather was icy cold, freezing her to the very marrow, in spite of her violent exertion. Up to now, she had not been able to make a dent in the chunk she had tackled. We'll see who is the master, she said to herself, gritting her teeth. She set the chunk on the block once more and, raising the ax high in the air, she brought it down on the flat side of the chunk with a mighty blow. The blade stuck in the wood this time. Again Margit raised the ax, which now brought the chunk along with it. Again and again she tried, and each time the blade sank a little deeper.

If I have to keep on all day, Margit thought savagely, I'm going to split this thing!

The chunk seemed to grow heavier and heavier with each blow, and the ax more difficult to wield. In a desperate attempt to finish the job, she raised both ax and chunk so high that she lost her balance. The ax slipped from her grasp and Margit found herself sprawling on her back on the ground. She picked herself up, brushed the snow off her dress and shawl, recovered the ax, still clinging to the obstinate chunk, and stationed herself before the chopping block once more.

She was just about to raise her ax, when she heard someone say, "That's no job for a girl." At the same time she felt someone take the ax handle away from her.

She turned around. Rolf Nordland stood just behind her.

"That's no work for a girl," he said again.

"It's—it's only that this chunk is so obstinate—it's so full of knots that it won't—it won't let itself be cut in two," Margit gasped.

Rolf brushed her aside and without another word gave the ax a quick twist, sending the chunk rolling in two parts in opposite directions.

Margit had not seen Rolf since the morning of Christmas Eve. Ever since then, the struggle for survival had been so difficult for everyone in the Kendall Colony that it had blotted out thought of all else.

There had been colds and more severe illness, first among the grownups and then the children. Fresh mounds in the new burial ground marked the graves of those who had not been able to withstand the rigors of frontier life. Master Cleng, his sister Carrie Nelson and Margit were the only three in the entire colony who had escaped illness. Carrie Nelson had cared for the very smallest children and their mothers and the most seriously ill and the dying in Master Cleng's cabin. Margit had done her best to keep things going in the community house. Master Cleng in some way had managed to procure enough food to prevent all of them from starving.

As the older boys recovered, they were sent immediately to the closest farms to work for flour, potatoes and any other food obtainable. The men, almost before they were able, went into the forests, because wood was needed for fuel and for lumber. Master Cleng had insisted on a new community store-house at once. And, he said, the sooner the cabins could be built, the better chances everyone would have to regain his health. Even after those Carrie Nelson was caring for had left the community house, it was still so overcrowded, Master Cleng declared, that relief must come at the earliest possible moment.

By the end of January, enough of the women had recovered sufficiently to take over the housekeeping duties and care for those who were still sick. Free at last, Margit had volunteered to split wood and do any other outdoor work. Today her wood chopping had not been very successful!

"What did you do to make the chunk split?" Margit asked.

Rolf did not answer. Instead, he picked up another chunk, poised the ax in the air and, with one stroke, sent its blade completely through the chunk. Then, holding one of the halves in his hand, he deftly cut it into sticks that Margit knew would exactly fit into the firebox of the stove. Rolf tackled one chunk after the other until a good-sized pile of firewood lay beside the block.

As Margit stood watching him, she thought he was the handsomest boy she had ever seen. A few strands of blond hair had escaped from the red knit cap he was wearing. His deep blue eyes were so clear and alert that they seemed to take in everything around him at a single glance.

Finally Rolf laid down the ax. "There," he said, "that should last you over night at least. What other chores have you taken upon your shoulders for today?"

Margit blushed. She wasn't sure whether he was in earnest or just trying to tease her. But she couldn't worry about either. There was too much that she needed desperately to accomplish.

"We need water for cooking," she said. "We melt snow

for the washing, but the men haven't had time to get down to the brook to cut a few blocks of ice."

Rolf picked up the ax. "Lead the way," he said crisply.

Margit ran over to the house first and brought the big flat sled Master Cleng had made. Then the two started out.

"The boys called you 'Margit' when we went to fetch the Christmas tree," Rolf said. "But I've never heard your family name. Whose daughter are you?"

"I'm not anyone's daughter," Margit said. Then realizing how ridiculous this must have sounded, she added, "At least not anyone's here in the colony."

"But you came over with the others, didn't you?" Rolf asked.

Margit blushed even more deeply. Could someone have told him of her arrival in America as a stowaway? She had hoped this episode would be entirely erased from everyone's memory by now. Was this young man prying? She doubted it. There was something about Rolf which made her realize that his questioning was not malicious. He only wanted to know more about her.

"I was brought up on the estate Master Cleng came from in Norway," Margit said. "He was my godfather. My parents died soon after I was christened."

"Then you're an orphan like me," Rolf said. "I came from the far north of Norway. My parents were fishermen. During a winter storm, our boat capsized and I was the only one who came out of it alive."

He was silent after that and Margit, in spite of her curiosity, decided not to ask questions. Rolf took such long steps that she had a hard time keeping up with him. Suddenly he stopped. "Here, why don't you sit on the sled and I'll pull you?"

"How can you find your way to the brook?"

"You can direct me, can't you?"

Again Margit was abashed by his abrupt manner. But his suggestion did make sense.

Finally they reached the brook. For some time after that, Rolf focused all his attention on the task at hand—marking off squares on the ice, cutting them swiftly but carefully so that they came out as solid cubes. Then he loaded the ice on the sled in two layers.

"I'm afraid you're going to have to walk back," he said.

"I don't mind," Margit assured him. Then, smiling, she said, "I'd really rather not have to sit on ice."

Rolf burst into hearty laughter. It was like music to Margit's ears. For a month now, there had not been a single wholehearted peal of laughter in the entire colony. But there had been more sobbing and desperate praying than she had heard in all her life.

"Do you often do that?" Margit asked.

"Do what?" Rolf asked.

"Laugh aloud."

Rolf regarded Margit in surprise. "Is there anything so unusual about having a good laugh?"

"In America there is. At least in the Kendall Colony. When we first came up here, it seemed fun. But now for a long time, things have been so bad I had almost forgotten there was laughter in the world."

"That's a terrible conclusion for a pretty young girl like you to have arrived at. I heard there had been a great deal of illness and some deaths in the colony. That was why I came over here to see if you needed help. I work at the Careys' farm, you remember."

"I began to believe that the evil trolls in Norway had followed us over here and were bringing all these disasters to punish us."

Again Rolf burst out laughing. Then he sobered. "Why should the evil trolls want to bring disasters down on you people?" he asked.

Margit hesitated. "When Master Cleng returned from America, he was very enthusiastic about the opportunities this new country had to offer. Conditions were difficult in Norway for many people, he said, and he tried to get some of them to migrate. Most of all, he urged Mistress Catherine, his wife. But she told him that God put people in that place in the world where He meant them to be, and that anyone who went against His wishes in this respect was tempting Providence. She believed, too, that trolls were always ready to punish human beings for their misdeeds."

There was a smile of amusement in Rolf's blue eyes. But this time he did not laugh aloud. He walked beside Margit in silence for a few minutes. Then, as if he had thought something through very carefully, he said, "According to that line of reasoning, the entire human race ought to be huddled together on the top of Mount Ararat. For it was there, you remember, that Noah and his family found themselves at the end of the flood."

This time it was Margit's turn to laugh. "I wonder what Mistress Catherine would have had to say, if Master Cleng had reminded her of that," she said. "She knew her Bible from cover to cover, and she could prove everything she said by quoting from it."

"According to Mistress Catherine's logic, my family should have been spared from drowning," Rolf said. "None of them had ever been off the tiny island where we lived except to embark in their fishing vessel. But they would have starved to death much earlier if they had remained on land."

Margit turned over in her mind what Rolf had said. Then

suddenly she asked, "How did you happen to come to America?"

"There was nothing to keep me any longer in Norway, trolls or no trolls. The extreme northern part of Norway is so close to Sweden that it was simple enough for me to walk across the border. I found that if I got to Gothenburg, there would be plenty of freighters on which I could work my way to America. You see, Cleng Peerson wasn't the only person who brought back glowing descriptions of the Promised Land. And I strained my ears to learn everything I could about it."

"Did you get to Gothenburg and find a freighter?"

"Sure. The boat I hired out on stopped at several ports, but it finally landed safely in New York harbor."

"You told me how you happened to come to America, but how did you happen to work for the Careys?"

"I went to Rochester to look for work and I happened to meet Mr. Carey. He was looking for someone to work on his place and he hired me."

"And has it been worth all the trouble?" Margit asked.

"Of course. The Careys are wonderful people to work for."

"I suppose you'll stay on with them," Margit said.

"For the present, yes. But this is only a start. I hope to get land of my own some day."

One of the blocks of ice fell off. They stopped and Rolf replaced it on the sled.

After they had been walking for some time, Rolf asked suddenly, "If Mistress Catherine was so much against migration, how did you and Cleng Peerson manage to get away?"

Now it was here again, Margit thought. Yet, after all, Rolf had been frank about his own story. But he hadn't anything to hide.

"Mistress Catherine didn't give her consent, even though in most things she was the boss on the estate. Master Cleng always traveled, as far back as I can remember. He had been in England, Germany, France and, I think, in other countries. So Mistress Catherine took it as a matter of course that he should leave for America."

"And you? Did he get her to consent to take you along?"

"Master Cleng forgot his notebook with valuable notes he had made about America on an earlier visit. Since I knew he would need them, I made up my mind to see that it was delivered personally to him."

"Whew! What a decision for a girl back in Norway to make!"

"Oh, I didn't intend at first to be the one to deliver it. I thought of Lars Larson. But when I got to Stavanger and saw the *Restoration*—"

"You managed somehow to board it and stayed there."

"Yes. Now you know the terrible truth. I came over as a stowaway. And so I have been wondering—perhaps I am the one who has brought all this ill luck to the Kendall Colony."

Rolf Nordland stopped and took Margit by the arm. "Listen, you silly goose," he said, "you've gotten yourself into a complete spider web of thinking. And I am going to free you from it right now. The worst you probably did while aboard was to eat part of the rations the ship carried. Since no one evidently starved, you need have no further worries on that score. I'm sure that, in some way, you did something to repay your keep, didn't you?"

"There wasn't much I could do but amuse the children."

"That was a lot. And since you arrived—well, from what I have seen today, you can't have been too great a burden to the group."

"Well—I—things just had to be done."

"Exactly. And you have done them and are doing them. But listen to what I am going to say. It is just as wrong carrying guilt in one's heart, when there is no occasion for it, as it is to do wrong in other ways. Remember, we are all God's creatures. Failing to treat ourselves as charitably as we would others is sin, too." Then a smile broke over his face. "Now I have been speaking like a preacher and that's the last thing I am fitted for. But you needed to be set right about this, and there seemed to be no one else except me to do it."

By this time they had arrived at the door of the community house. Rolf unloaded the ice blocks and chopped one of them into small pieces ready to be taken into the house and melted.

"I must be going now," he said when he had finished. "The Careys will be wondering what has kept me. But from now on, I'll drop over once in a while to see that you don't do any backsliding in your thinking. As for the colony, I know it will turn out to be a successful one. Cleng Peerson is a very clever man and has such drive that he will direct the activities of everyone until each family gets on its own. It's only for the present that things have been rather hard."

"I don't know how to thank you," Margit said.

"That's easy. Don't tackle any more obstinate chunks of wood, and leave the ice hauling to the men."

That evening, long after Margit had rolled herself into her quilt on the floor, she lay awake. She had never met anyone like Rolf Nordland. Master Cleng, to be sure, resembled him, but he was older and didn't understand as Rolf did how a young girl felt. Suddenly the joy of being in America returned to her, and again she felt a tingle of anticipation and curiosity about all the wonderful things that were in store for her. For Margit was free now. Free of the burden of guilt, which she had felt because of the suffering and trouble in the colony ever since the fire. Rolf had made her see how wrong she had been to think that what had happened was meant as a punishment for her. She folded her hands and thanked God for sending Rolf Nordland.

CHAPTER SIXTEEN

Margit stroked the folds in the skirt of her new dress. It was her first new article of clothing since her arrival in the Kendall Colony. It had been a present from Mrs. Carey, who had taken it from her own wardrobe and helped Margit alter it to fit her. Mrs. Carey and Margit had become very friendly since Rolf Nordland had taken her over to call on the Careys. But the dress had been a secret—her appearance in it today would be a complete surprise to everyone.

It was late in October and since the weather was especially warm for this time of year her new dress of soft wool might have been considered too warm. But there was to be a quilting bee this afternoon, and she was determined to wear it, no matter what the weather.

During the late summer and fall, there had been a series of quilting bees in the settlement. Just as the men got together to put up each family cabin, so the women gathered and spent a day helping the homemaker who was to move into her new home. This was to be the last of the quilting bees, at least for the present, for the Rossedahls were the last family to move into their own cabin. Margit would be left alone in the community house.

"Your dress is very becoming," Mrs. Rossedahl told Margit.

"Thank you," Margit said. "Mrs. Carey gave it to me, you know. It was one of her own and she helped me remodel it. I learned a lot about sewing from her."

"You are fortunate," Mrs. Rossedahl said. "A needle is one of a homemaker's best friends. I only wish I had had the patience to learn more when my mother was trying to teach me. It would have made things easier for me now."

The two started out together for the quilting bee.

"We're late," Mrs. Rossedahl said, beginning to walk faster as she spoke. "The women will be waiting for me to tell them how I want the quilts stitched."

"A few minutes more or less won't matter," Margit told her. "It's so beautiful outside that I wish we didn't have to go into the house at all," she added as they walked down the narrow path leading to the Rossedahl cabin.

"It's really unbelievable that it's only a year since we arrived in the colony," Mrs. Rossedahl said. "Here are fields on both sides of us, brown with the stubble after harvesting our first crop. Except for Cleng Peerson's plot, not a single foot of ground in the settlement had been broken with a plow when we arrived and not a grain of seed had been planted."

"And on each plot there is a cabin and other buildings, too," Margit reminded her. "When Master Cleng returned to Norway after his first stay in America and told such amazing tales about the new land, Mistress Catherine wouldn't believe him. She ought to be here now to see for herself."

"Yes, we really have Cleng Peerson to thank for everything," Mrs. Rossedahl said. "After the storehouse fire, things certainly looked hopeless. And even worse later with so much sickness and so many deaths. I used to think he was pretty hard on the boys, making them go to work on the farms around here. And he kept the men out in the woods in weather that would freeze fire. But I guess he knew what he was doing."

"There wouldn't have been food last winter and seed for planting and lumber for all the buildings in the settlement, if he hadn't," Margit said.

"And the queer part of it was that all the time he was driving everybody to the limit, you wouldn't have known that he had a thought in his head. He went around laughing and joking and the way he talked while he was parceling out the hardest jobs, you'd have thought he was inviting us to play a game with him."

"It really was a game, wasn't it, Mrs. Rossedahl? One at which we could all win—at least those of you who had families."

"Well, I know that if it hadn't been for Cleng Peerson, my husband and I would have packed up our children and left," Mrs. Rossedahl admitted.

"Are you sorry you didn't?" Margit asked.

"Of course not," Mrs. Rossedahl said shortly.

They walked on in silence for a while. The sun was so warm, the sky so blue and the air so fragrant with the smell of dried grass and freshly turned earth that Margit drank it all in as if she couldn't get enough of the beauty around her.

After a sharp turn in the trail, Mrs. Rossedahl exclaimed, "What a crowd of children outside our cabin! Most of the people must have arrived ahead of us." She started walking so fast she was almost running and Margit found it hard to keep up with her.

Carrie Nelson was outside the cabin to greet them. From a distance, Margit heard her say, "Mrs. Rossedahl, we have been waiting for you to tell us how you want the quilts stitched. Everyone is eager to begin."

Inside the cabin, women were seated on planks around two quilt frames. Even though the cabin was larger than most of the others, there was little space left for anything else.

"We carried your things outside to allow more room in here," Carrie Nelson told Mrs. Rossedahl. "We thought your family would be needing plenty of bedding and we could quilt more by working on two at the same time."

"I see you've started already," Mrs. Rossedahl said.

"Yes, the material is stretched on both frames, the wool bats laid in place, the covers put on, and we've even basted them down. So now we can start stitching as soon as you give us your directions," Carrie Nelson told her.

Margit sat on the end of a plank in a corner of the room. Soon all the women were stitching busily, and the only sound was the clicking of scissors and the breaking of thread. Suddenly Margit became aware of a low conversation at the opposite end of the room.

"I wonder what he'll do with the place, now that the Rossedahls are moving out."

"You know that she—" The rest was spoken too softly for Margit to hear.

"Oh, it won't be standing empty for long. Cleng Peerson wants Norwegian families to settle on every plot of ground that is left."

"Didn't someone say he went to Rochester this morning?"

"Yes, it was supposed to be to visit the Lars Larsons. You know Lars is already doing well building boats for the new canal."

"I heard that he went to see if he could get work for—"

The speaker looked in Margit's direction and did not finish the sentence.

Margit began to feel very uncomfortable. She bent over her work and pretended to be concentrating on that alone.

"Now that we all have separate homes of our own, he can't really expect us to—"

Margit was growing more embarrassed by the minute.

"I thought maybe he might—"

The air in the cabin was becoming unbearable.

"Of course, if that widow should come here. She's been quite sick, and he might want her to stay on to help out—"

Again one of the women looked in Margit's direction.

"Yes. She's really good at working. Much better than I thought she'd be."

"She certainly pitched in while things were at their worst last winter, you'll have to admit."

The women around Margit's quilt had begun to talk, too. Soon there was an unintelligible buzzing of voices throughout the room. Margit felt her cheeks and ears burn.

Finally she got up and walked over to the stove where Carrie Nelson was watching coffee kettles. "I thought maybe you'd like to have me go out and see how the children are getting along," Margit said.

"That will be fine," Carrie Nelson told her. "You are so good with them. There are several horses out there, and even though they are tied to trees, I'd feel easier with an older person to keep an eye on things."

As Margit stepped outside, she heaved a sigh of relief. The air in the cabin had become unbearably hot and stuffy. Not since she had listened to the passengers on the *Restoration* argue about how she was to be fed while crossing the Atlantic had she felt so miserable. It was queer that now, when each family had its own home and plenty of provisions to last through the winter, she seemed to have become so much more of a burden to them than while they had been absolutely destitute.

Suddenly the children saw her and swarmed around her.

"Oh, Margit, tell us a story," they all cried in a chorus. "Tell us about the kind Indian girl that told the other Indians that they couldn't kill the white man."

"You've heard the story of Pocahontas a hundred times," Margit said. "But all right. I'll sit on this stump and all of you come close to me, so I won't disturb the ladies inside the cabin."

The children squatted down on the ground around her, eager to have her begin. It wasn't easy for her to keep her mind on her story, but she did her best and the children listened eagerly as if they had never heard it before. They clamored for more, but just then Carrie Nelson came out of the cabin.

"We're serving coffee now," she said. Her tone was unusually gentle, and Margit suspected that she had either heard a part of the women's conversation or had been told about it.

"I'm not hungry," Margit said. "When you get ready to feed the children, why don't you let me serve them out here? If I want anything then, I can eat with them."

"As you wish," Carrie Nelson said and disappeared into the cabin.

The cabin was casting a shadow much longer than its height by the time the last hungry child had been fed. Margit carried the dishes into the cabin. She saw quilts stitched and finished at the edges, folded and carefully piled on top of a stump. And the fingers of the women around the frames were busily working on others.

"You people seem to have Mrs. Rossedahl's quilting almost done," Margit said, "so I don't think I'll be needed here any more."

Carrie Nelson was busily washing dishes and preparing for the evening meal when the men and boys would also be there. "Yes, they're on the last quilts," Carrie Nelson said.

"Then I think I'll go back to the community house, if you don't mind," Margit said.

"But we're serving such a good supper. And I promised Brother Cleng, when he left for Rochester this morning, to take you back with us and have you stay overnight with us in our cabin."

"That isn't necessary," Margit said. "Besides, now that everyone has moved out, it will need a good going over."

"But aren't you afraid to stay there alone?"

"Of course not. What is there to be afraid of?"

"Well," Carrie Nelson said hesitatingly, "I suppose there isn't anything. And there are cabins not too far away. But I don't think Brother Cleng is going to like my allowing you to stay there all the same."

"You can tell him to blame me," Margit said.

"Anyway, if you should change your mind or get lonely," Carrie Nelson said, "remember you are welcome to come to our cabin at any time."

"Thank you," Margit said.

But Margit was resolved that if she was frightened out of her wits, she wouldn't leave. She would show the members of the colony that she was old enough to look after herself. They would not have to worry about her becoming a burden to any of them.

As she retraced her steps over the trail, the landscape looked entirely different. The stubble in the harvested fields had lost its golden gleam, the green of the pine trees was duller and the buildings, darkened by the deep shadows around them, no longer reflected warmth and love from within. It was a relief to reach the community house.

With the setting of the sun, the air had grown chilly, so Margit closed the door. Since only a suggestion of light came in through the single window, the room was dark and gloomy. Margit went over to the stove and on the shelf close by she found a few matches and a candle that had been left behind. She lit the candle and set it on the shelf. The flickering light, though far from making the room cheerful, helped a little to dispel the dreariness of the place.

Then Margit took off her new dress and hung it carefully on its peg. As she stood admiring it, she suddenly realized that not a single person at the quilting bee had made a remark about it. In her misery of the afternoon, she had not missed their compliments. Yet for weeks she had gloated over the surprise her beautiful dress was going to give them when she appeared in it.

A huge yellow moon was slowly rising above the horizon and sending its rays through the window. The light from the candle had grown steadier, too. The room no longer seemed dark and depressing. Margit looked around, pivoting on her heels, and taking in every detail of the place at a single glance. Most of the bunks around the walls were entirely empty, except for some dilapidated mattresses out of which wisps of straw were leaking. In her own bunk alone, the bedding remained intact, showing that it would be occupied. On the shelf above the stove stood a few cracked dishes, some odds and ends of food and a very sooty copper kettle. An odd red mitten, a crock of sour milk and a rusty fork on the table had either been forgotten or discarded by their owners. The floor was littered with scraps of paper, remnants of frayed rope and stale straw that had escaped from the mattresses. Even during the most crowded days in the community house, the place had never been in such a state of neglect.

Yet, as Margit looked around her, she felt a lightness and

real happiness, such as she had never experienced in all her life. It had suddenly come to her that, at the moment at least, she was the absolute mistress of her own establishment. There was no one to tell her what to do or when to do it. No one to please. She could do what she liked whenever she had the notion to do it. No princess living in the finest palace was as free as she was right now.

Margit started walking around the room, surveying her domain. She began to hum a tune and soon she was keeping step with the tune. She moved faster and faster. Her humming changed to lively singing. Finally Margit lifted her petticoat and whirled around the room in a dizzy, breath-taking dance. She kept on until she was completely exhausted and she sank down in a state of utter ecstasy on the stool which, during her dancing, she had pushed into a corner.

After she had somewhat recovered, the thought of her new freedom was so exciting that Margit decided to make the very most of it while it lasted. She would set her house in order. Even though she was permitted to rule over it for only a short while, she would make it as neat and as pleasant as possible. She would show the housewives in the settlement that she could hold her own with the best of them. If the family which Master Cleng was supposed to bring back with him should arrive in the morning, she had no time to lose. She would see to it that he could be proud of the place.

Margit went into action. She emptied the old straw into the stove, since it would serve as kindling. She would need hot water to scrub the bunks, the shelves, the table, the stump chair and the floor. She would wash the cracked dishes, too, the rusty fork and the odd red mitten. There was still wood in the box and soon she had a lively fire going and the copper kettle, already scoured so it shone, was steaming.

Margit discarded everything on the shelves that was unusable. It was surprising how attractive the shelf looked with the clean, cracked dishes arranged beside the polished candle holder with its candle still burning steadily and the brown crock out of which she had cleaned the sour milk. She washed the window inside and out and then she indulged in an orgy of scrubbing. By the time she had finished, the stove had cooled, and she gave it such an overhauling that, except for the remnants of ashes in the firebox, it might have been taken for new.

Breathless, but still in a state of exhilaration, Margit sat down on the stump that served as the only chair and surveyed her handiwork. She was satisfied. Mistress Catherine herself could not have found fault with a single detail.

Margit washed her hands and face, combed her hair and put on her new blue dress once more in order to look the part of the mistress of her own establishment. Then she heard footsteps just outside the door. She was startled and for a moment, frightened. Perhaps Master Cleng and Carrie Nelson had been right about her not staying in the house overnight by herself. There were more footsteps. Then a knock at the door.

Margit's first impulse was to cry out. There was no lock, so she could not prevent whoever was there from entering. But no. She was the mistress of this establishment. She was a mature woman. She would act like one. Shaking inwardly, but maintaining as much outward calm as she could manage, Margit walked slowly toward the door. For an instant, she stood irresolute. Then she took a firm hold of the latch and pulled it. In the doorway, with the moonlight shining on his blond hair, stood Rolf Nordland.

"They told me you had come back here," he said. "Carrie Nelson had invited me to come to supper with the men at the Rossedahl cabin."

Margit was too surprised to speak. Then she remembered her manners. She was the mistress now. "Won't—won't you come in?" she faltered.

There was only the one stump chair, and since neither hostess nor guest could very well sit on the floor in a well-run establishment, Margit and Rolf sat down on the stump together. And since the polite hostess sat at the very edge of the chair to leave most of it for the guest, the thoughtful guest, fearing she might fall, put his arm around her. And the two sat there in beautiful silence, for how long, neither of them knew.

Finally Rolf turned so that he could look down into Margit's face. "Do you know that the color of your dress exactly matches your eyes?" he said softly.

"Do you like it? I mean the dress."

"It's very lovely."

"It's the very first new dress I've had since coming to the settlement. Mrs. Carey gave it to me."

"Suppose I should tell you that I know a person who would like to supply you with pretty dresses for the rest of your life—what would you say?"

"It—it would depend on who the person was."

"If at this moment he was in this room?"

Margit felt her heart beat wildly. "Then—then—I'd—I'd like it very much."

Rolf bent down and kissed Margit gently.

The silence which followed was longer than the kiss and even more beautiful.

It was much later that Rolf said, "Listen, Margit. Your Master Cleng says that the future for young Americans lies in the West. He's thinking of making a tour out there to investigate conditions for a new settlement. I'd love to go, too, but only on one condition."

"And that is?"

"That you go with me."

This time Rolf read his answer in Margit's eyes.

At last he took his leave. After he was gone, Margit, still wearing her new blue dress, sat on the stump and dreamed. It would be a beautiful home in the West, which she and Rolf Nordland would build together. They and their American children would live happily in it for the rest of their lives. Not even a queen, presiding over her entire kingdom, was ever as fortunate as she was now and would be to the end of her days.